Molly

and the

Gambler

Molly and the Gambler

Stephen Overholser

Thorndike Press • Chivers Press
Waterville, Maine USA Bath, England

This Large Print edition is published by Thorndike Press, USA and by Chivers Press, England.

Published in 2001 in the U.S. by arrangement with Golden West Literary Agency.

Published in 2001 in the U.K. by arrangement with Golden West Literary Agency.

U.S. Hardcover 0-7862-3611-6 (Western Series Edition)
U.K. Hardcover 0-7540-4716-4 (Chivers Large Print)
U.K. Softcover 0-7540-4717-2 (Camden Large Print)

The text of this Large Print edition is unabridged.
Other aspects of the book may vary from the original edition.

Set in 16 pt. Plantin by Christina S. Huff.

Printed in the United States on permanent paper.

British Library Cataloguing-in-Publication Data available

Library of Congress Cataloging-in-Publication Data

Overholser, Stephen.
    Molly and the gambler / Stephen Overholser.
       p. cm.
    ISBN 0-7862-3611-6 (lg. print : hc : alk. paper)
    1. Undercover operations — Fiction. 2. Colorado —
Fiction. 3. Gamblers — Fiction. 4. Large type books.
    I. Title.
PS3565.V43 M56 2001
  813'.54—dc21   2001041558

Molly and the Gambler

I

Molly had seen the sleight-of-hand trick before, and now from her seat in the rocking passenger coach of the northbound train she watched as the cardsharp pulled it on the young cowhand.

The smooth-cheeked young man sat in the upholstered chair beside Molly, his cowhide suitcase balanced on his knees, and when he wasn't looking out at the Colorado scenery sliding past the window, he faced the cardsharp in the opposite chair. Molly had observed this skeletal man as he had passed through the car and then come back to that particular seat. He'd found his mark.

Gaunt and in need of a shave, the cardsharp was dressed in a black pinstriped suit, white shirt, and string tie. The cuffs of his shirt were grimy and his suit was threadbare at the elbows and knees. But he had a ready smile and he struck up a friendly conversation, soon learning that the young man was traveling alone, headed for a wrangling job on a ranch a few miles outside of Cheyenne, Wyoming.

The challenge was made in a harmless, good-natured way. When it was accepted, a bony hand drew out a sealed deck of cards from a coat pocket. The cardsharp broke the seal, tore off the wrapping, and fanned out the cards to show that all fifty-two were there. Turning the deck over, he began shuffling, keeping up his steady banter all the while.

"Five dollars says that I can turn up the queen of hearts with the first cut," he said, squaring the deck. He set it on the flat side of the young man's suitcase. "Yessir, with the first cut I'll turn up the queen of my heart."

The young cowhand cast a skeptical look at him. "Not after I've shuffled them, you won't."

The cardsharp pursed his thin lips, feigning reluctance to go through with it. "Well, you've got me there." He paused. "All right, go ahead. Mix them up a bit."

The young cowhand grinned and reached for the deck.

"But first," the cardsharp said, "let me see the color of your money." In his hand appeared a crisp five-dollar bill.

The young man leaned back and dug into the pocket of his denim trousers. He pulled out some crumpled bills and smoothed out five ones on the suitcase. Then he picked up the deck. He had obviously handled playing cards before, probably in bunkhouse penny-ante games, and now he riffled them repeatedly.

"You're going to wear those pasteboards out," the cardsharp complained.

"You said mix them up," he replied, grinning, "and I aim to do a proper job of it." With a last flourish the young cowhand squared the cards and set the deck between them.

The cardsharp leaned forward. He stared at the cards as though in deep concentration. Then he slowly reached out with his left hand. He made the cut, passing the half-deck to his right hand in one smooth motion. When he turned over that half of the deck, the red queen was there.

"The queen of my heart," he said, eyeing the young man.

Molly saw the cowhand's face color. After a long moment he pushed the five dollars across the flat side of the leather suitcase toward the man. Then, sensing he'd been cheated, he suddenly grabbed the cards and flipped through them.

"You can have that deck," the cardsharp said, pocketing the wrinkled dollar bills. "You'll find that they're honest cards."

Jaw clenched, the young man made no reply. His face was beet red as he held the cards in one hand, undoubtedly the most expensive deck he'd ever bought.

"I don't believe you can do that twice in a row," Molly said.

The cardsharp's beady eyes flickered in surprise. "Well now, you might be right about that, ma'am."

"I'll put up five dollars to find out," she said.

"Pretty lady like you don't seem like the gambling type," he said.

"Don't try it," the young cowhand warned her. "He's got some kind of trick —"

"That wasn't a trick, sonny," the cardsharp said, "and don't you be accusing me of dishonesty."

Molly smiled at the young man. "Both of my eyes are open." She drew a five-dollar bill out of her handbag and held it out to the gaunt man. "I suppose you have another deck in your pocket."

"As it happens, I do," the cardsharp replied. He produced a deck that was identical to the first one and said with a smile, "Seal unbroken until this very moment."

Molly watched him break the seal and unwrap the cards. He fanned them open so she could see the queen of hearts. Then he began his banter as he shuffled them several times.

"Care to mix them up yourself, ma'am?" he asked, setting the deck on the flat side of the suitcase.

Molly shook her head. "Go ahead. Cut them."

Again the cardsharp fixed his gaze on the deck, as though concentrating on where the queen was. The moment his left hand hovered over the deck, Molly reached out and grasped his right wrist.

He looked up in surprise. "What're you doing?"

"It only takes one hand to cut the deck," she said. "Make your cut."

His expression darkened. "Turn loose of me."

"She's right," the cowhand said with growing excitement. "You can cut that deck with one hand."

The cardsharp glowered at them and withdrew his left hand. He tried to pull back from Molly's grasp, but she held him fast.

"What's wrong, mister?" the cowhand asked.

When he didn't reply, Molly bent his wrist around. She plucked a card from his hand and tossed it onto the suitcase, face up. It was the queen of hearts.

The young cowhand's eyes widened. "You palmed that queen . . . right under my eyes. It *was* a trick!"

Molly said, "He fans the deck open not to show you where the queen of hearts is, but so he'll know. Then as he cuts the deck to shuffle, he palms it."

"So it didn't matter how many times I mixed them up," the young cowhand exclaimed. "The queen wasn't even there!"

His gaunt face set in anger, the cardsharp made a move to leave.

"After you've returned this gentleman's money," Molly said, "I won't hold you to our wager."

With a look of utter disdain, the cardsharp dropped a five-dollar bill on the suitcase. He stood and walked away, heading for the smoking car.

After sundown the passenger train nosed into Cheyenne. Molly climbed down from the coach amid the other passengers, including a grateful young cowhand, now wiser. He had learned a valuable lesson about cardsharps who worked the trains. With a last good-bye and a handshake, they parted.

Valise in hand, Molly left the depot and crossed the street to the Plains Hotel. She checked into an upstairs room and changed out of her traveling dress. She rested, and then after a late supper in the hotel dining room, a hack took her to the Stockmen's Inn on the north edge of town.

By moonlight Molly saw the private club. A two-story building with a peaked roof, it stood alone on a grassy knoll. Curtained windows glowed warmly with the light of oil lamps. The hack pulled up at the steps of the veranda, and out of the shadows came an armed man.

"Members only," he said, leaning into the hack.

"Dave Hughes is expecting me. I'm Molly Owens."

Without another word, the guard shifted his cut-down shotgun from one hand to the other and helped Molly down. He took her up the half-dozen steps and they crossed the veranda to the front door.

The door was opened by a slight, soft-spoken butler in a brass-buttoned uniform. After a whispered word from the guard, Molly was admitted to a dimly lit hallway.

Cigar smoke, deep laughter, and the light *clink* of crystal glasses greeted her as she was led down the hall past closed doors to a back parlor. The butler pulled aside a heavy curtain and Molly stepped inside.

She entered a Persian-carpeted, luxuriously furnished gaming room where well-dressed gentlemen stood at three roulette wheels or sat around felt-covered tables where poker, faro, or three-card monte were dealt. The civilized atmosphere was punctuated by rich laughter from a winner at one of the tables, followed by a deep-voiced call for another round of drinks from the cherry-wood bar at the back of the room. Molly looked over there and saw shapely young women with silver trays in hand.

"Mr. Hughes is back there, ma'am."

Molly followed the butler's gaze. At a poker table she saw a broad-shouldered man wearing a gray Prince Albert coat and silk shirt. His beard was full, streaked with silver, and his sandy hair was combed back from his forehead and curled neatly at the back of his neck. A handsome man, Molly guessed he was in his late forties.

She recognized the breed. Dave Hughes was a professional gambler. And, judging by the surroundings, he was one who had earned a good reputation. The Stockmen's Inn drew wealthy ranchers from Wyoming, Nebraska, Kansas, and Colorado, as well as railroad barons, shipping magnates, and eastern financiers who arrived in Cheyenne in their private railcars. *No sleight-of-hand artists or marked-card shysters here,* Molly thought as she crossed the room to Hughes's table, *just as there would be no watered whiskey at the bar or cheap women in the rooms upstairs.*

Dave Hughes was dealing five-card draw to four men dressed in crisply tailored suits. The gambler possessed the air of self-assurance essential to his trade, and now Molly watched him deal the cards.

Hand movements smooth and economical, Hughes dealt with seeming effortlessness. Every blue-backed card landed exactly where the gambler aimed, making a neat stack in front of each player.

Molly circled the table while bets were placed. Chips softly clicked together as they were tossed into the center of the green felt-covered table. New cards were called for, and Hughes swiftly dealt them.

After another round of betting and raising, Dave Hughes folded and sat back while the hand was played out. A cigar-smoking man with a curled, waxed mustache won the pot, and casually scooped up more than three hundred dollars' worth of chips. Hughes's gaze swept past the grinning winner, and that was the moment Molly caught his eye.

"Gentlemen," Hughes said, pushing back his chair, "if you'll excuse me." As he stood, he signaled for another dealer.

"Cards gone cold on you, Dave?" one of the men asked, chuckling.

The winner of the pot said, "I liked the way you dealt that last hand."

"I didn't," grumbled a third man, as he trimmed the end off a fresh cigar.

Hughes said, "Time for a new dealer, I'd say." He picked up his winnings and moved around the table to Molly.

"Miss Owens?" he asked.

She nodded.

Hughes took her by the arm. "I have a room upstairs where we can talk."

As she was led across the room past the spinning roulette wheels, Molly said, "You were holding the winning hand. Not many men would fold a full house, ace high."

Hughes cast a quick grin at her. "I picked up two big pots earlier in the evening. If I win too often, I'm out of a job." He took her to a private door behind the cherrywood bar. They stepped into a back hall. Molly saw that it led to the kitchen in one direction and a staircase in the other.

They mounted the staircase to the second floor of the Stockmen's Inn. The upstairs hall gave access to a series of rooms. Through one of the doors Molly heard a feminine shriek of delight, followed by a man's laughter, deep and satisfied. *Gentlemen's entertainment behind these locked doors,* Molly thought.

Hughes led the way. Down the hall he rounded the corner and strode to the last door. Molly waited behind him as he slid a key into the lock and opened it. He stepped inside, paused to light a lamp, then turned and invited her in.

"You lousy, two-timing bastard."

Startled, Hughes whirled around. A big, dark-haired woman lurched toward him, her face flushed. She wore a long dress of black silk, cut low over her breasts to show a deep cleavage. Her hand was clutched around the handle of a short-bladed knife, and now she cursed Hughes in a slurred voice.

"Jane," he said, raising a hand in front of him, "now, Janie —"

"You won't break the heart of another woman," she said the instant before she lunged, lashing out with the knife.

Hughes tried to spin away but hit the doorjamb. The point of the blade caught his coat sleeve and laid it open from elbow to wrist. He stared in shock as bright red blood seeped out and dripped from his elbow.

Intent on finishing the job, the woman made a second lunge, screeching this time. Hughes retreated before her onslaught.

Molly leaped forward, using both hands to grasp the wrist of the woman's knife hand and thrust the arm upward. They came together and for a moment stood face to face. Molly stared into the wildest pair of eyes she'd ever seen, and then shoved the big woman's arm to the side, twisting her wrist as she brought it down. A scream of pain stretched the woman's mouth open, and the knife clattered across the floor.

Molly glimpsed a blur of movement as the woman's other hand came slashing for her face like a claw. Instinctively, Molly raised her arm and blocked it. She drew back her fist and threw a short punch to the woman's throat.

Molly stepped back as the woman, gasping, doubled over and sank to her knees. She coughed and tried to draw a breath, her broad face turning deep red.

Molly turned around and saw Hughes in the hall. He clutched his arm, blood dripping onto the floor and the tops of his polished shoes. His gaze met Molly's.

"I reckon you've figured out by now," he said with half a smile, "that I have trouble with women."

II

The wound looked worse than it was. Molly pulled back the blood-soaked sleeves of Hughes's coat and silk shirt and saw a shallow cut on the underside of his arm. She led him past the gasping woman and into the room. A porcelain pitcher and basin stood on a washstand near the brass bed.

Molly washed the wound, then tore a towel to make a bandage. While she did so, the woman coughed and struggled to her feet. Holding a hand to her throat, she leaned against the doorjamb, breathing raggedly.

"First you take my man," she said hoarsely, "then you ruin my singing voice."

"You never had a singing voice," Hughes said.

She ignored him. "Look here, lady, if you think you're gonna take my man away from me, you'd damn well better think again —"

"Jane, I'm not your man," Hughes said.

"That ain't what you told me the other night when you got me into that bed," she said. "You two-timing bastard."

"Get out of here, Jane," Hughes said matter-of-factly, without taking his gaze from the bandage Molly fashioned. After she tied the last strip of towel, he moved swiftly to the door.

"He'll be two-timing you next," the woman said around a cough, "after he sweet-talks you until you can't see straight."

Disgusted, Hughes said, "You don't have any idea what you're talking about. Miss Owens is here on business —"

"Sure, just like that skinny chippie you slept with last night," she said.

Hughes reached out with his good arm and started to close the door.

"Damn right I'll leave," she said, backing away. "I can't stand the smell in here."

Hughes slammed the door and turned around. "You can see where she gets her nickname. Where there's trouble, there's Calamity."

A moment passed before Molly realized what he meant. "She's Calamity Jane?"

Hughes nodded. "Martha Jane Canary is her real name." He came to the bed and sat on the edge of it. "We've crossed trails in a lot of gambling halls over the years."

"She has a strong attachment to you," Molly said.

Hughes replied with a grimace, then dismissed the matter. "Jane's a big, strong woman. I don't know how you handled her, but you had her down in a flash. If it wasn't for you, she'd have opened me up like a can of beans. Now I know why Horace Fenton recommended you so highly as the right operative for this case."

"You want to talk about the case now?" Molly said. "I can wait until morning —"

"No, no," he said with a wave of his uninjured arm. "The sooner we get to it, the better. I suppose you know what the job is."

Molly nodded. "Yes, but I want to hear the details — everything you can tell me." Upon her acceptance of this case, Molly had received a packet of background information from the Fenton Investigative Agency in New York.

"Sharon, my daughter, ran away about seven, eight months ago," Hughes said. He paused. "Ran away. That isn't quite the right way to say it. She's no child. She's a young woman, going on eighteen. I reckon what I should say is that she left without telling me where she was going. She can take care of herself."

"But you want to help her?" Molly asked.

Hughes exhaled. "That's right." He reached into an inside pocket of his Prince Albert coat and brought out a thick roll of hundred-dollar bills. Gazing at the money, he continued, "I wasn't much of a father to Sharon. Years ago my wife died, and Sharon was raised by shirttail relatives. She lived with me off and on, and when I settled here in Cheyenne a couple of years ago, she moved in with me."

He paused, staring at the money in his hand. "We had our differences, mainly about the life I lead, and she got to talking about going off on her own. I tried to discourage her . . . a mistake on my part. The more I argued, the more determined she became. One morning when I was asleep she left." He looked at Molly, and the corners of his eyes were creased with sadness. "Just like that."

"But you know where she went," Molly said.

"Not until three weeks ago," Hughes replied. "A gambler came through and said he'd seen Sharon down in Creede. You know where that is?"

Molly nodded. Creede was a booming silver camp in the San Juan Mountains of southern Colorado. Denver newspaper accounts portrayed it as a tough, nearly lawless camp.

"Well," Hughes said, "at first I wanted to go after her. Figured I'd haul her out of there and talk some sense into her. But, hell,

I know that's nothing but a daydream. It wouldn't work."

He held out the roll of greenbacks. "Seventeen hundred dollars here. I won it on the turn of a card the day after I learned where Sharon had gone. One hundred dollars for every year of her life — whatever that means. But it seems like fate, doesn't it? Like this money was meant for her." He paused. "Anyhow, I want you to give it to her. Tell her it's from me. Tell her there's no strings attached to it. She doesn't have to come and see me or thank me or anything. I just want her to have a good start in life — better than the one I've given her so far."

Molly reached out and took the money from his hand. "You have a photographic portrait of her?"

Hughes shook his head. "Wish I did. But I don't think you'll have much trouble locating her. She's working in a gambling hall and saloon called the Orleans Club." He paused, running his hand over his full beard. "Sharon's about your height. Hair's the color of mine, and she has a strawberry birthmark at her throat." He added, "She's pretty, too."

Molly returned to her room in the Plains Hotel. This assignment was simple enough, but her interest had been caught by the man. Underneath his air of confidence and quiet good manners was a deep sadness. She suspected he was a man fleeing from his past, haunted by regrets.

She fell asleep thinking about him. In the pillow case under her head was the roll of hundred-dollar bills, and the fingers of her right hand curled around the pearl grips of her .38.

Early in the morning she boarded the southbound passenger train. Reaching Denver at noon, she caught a hack that took her to Capitol Hill and the graveled drive of Mrs. Boatwright's Boarding House for Ladies. Molly was met at the front door by the proprietress herself.

Mrs. Boatwright was a sturdy, well-dressed woman in her mid-fifties. Her angular features were not softened by her gray-streaked hair, which was braided and coiled at the back of her head like a crown. She was empress here, and looked the part.

"That was a fast trip to Cheyenne," she said as Molly came into the entryway. "Now I suppose you're off on another of your adventures."

Molly smiled in reply. Mrs. Boatwright had always expressed a mother's concern for her future — and relentless worry for the present.

"Not much of an adventure this time," Molly said. "I'm leaving for Creede tomorrow."

"Oh, I don't suppose you'll find any adventure in that camp full of thieves and killers," Mrs. Boatwright said.

Molly laughed. "I won't be there more than a few hours, just long enough to make a delivery. Then I'll turn around and come home. Mr. Fenton will probably have a new packet delivered by the time I return."

"A new way to get you maimed," Mrs. Boatwright said, "or worse." She shook her head. "I don't know why you do it, Molly. A beautiful young woman like you ought to be ready and waiting for that certain man."

"I keep my eyes open," Molly said.

"But you're a moving target," she said. "No man can keep you in his sights." Her brow furrowed. "Youthful beauty doesn't last forever."

"Then how do you account for yours?" Molly asked.

Mrs. Boatwright tried in vain to suppress a smile. "You're turning the tables on me, Molly Owens, when you ought to be listening to what I'm saying."

"I do listen," Molly said as she started up the carpeted staircase to her room.

"But you don't pay me any mind," the

landlady said after her.

Molly cast a smile back at her. That was true. Mrs. Boatwright firmly believed that a woman's purpose in life was to make herself available to a good man, marry him, serve him and bear his children. She clung to that belief still, even though a dozen years ago it had led to the greatest crisis of her life.

Upon the sudden death of her husband, Mrs. Boatwright learned from the family banker that the Boatwright fortune was gone. She inherited the Boatwright debt. And her banker told her that the only way to satisfy the creditors was to sell the mansion.

These were dark days, she confided to Molly. She knew nothing of business or investments, and had no idea of what plan her husband had had to recoup the fortune that had originally come from silver mines in Leadville. She had spent her time and energies with wifely duties, including huge parties in the mansion built by her husband, a great marble and stone building that had become a Denver landmark.

But she possessed a strong will, and decided that above all she must keep her home. She considered the skills she had acquired in handling everything from marketing and planning large parties to scheduling ice and coal deliveries. How could she use these skills?

Late one sleepless night an idea came to her. Ladies of means would much prefer to reside in a home than a hotel in the middle of town. She would start a boarding house.

The family banker was skeptical. But at last he agreed to go along with the plan. Success did not come instantly, or even in the first year, but in the third year a smile lined his thin face when Mrs. Boatwright began sending in double payments. Her instincts had been correct. Wealthy women flocked to her mansion and lived there while visiting in the Rockies, passing through, or in retirement.

Thinking of the irony that Mrs. Boatwright still believed women should rely entirely on men, when she herself had become successful on her own initiative, Molly went to her room and unpacked her valise. While her bath was being drawn, she undressed. Molly was full-breasted and supple, with a small waist curving out to her hips. She put on a robe, then checked over the tools of her profession that she carried in her handbag.

In the leather handbag was a ring of master skeleton keys, a set of lock probes made of watchspring steel, and her Colt Lightning Model .38 revolver. The gun had the stopping power at close range of a large-caliber weapon, yet with its short barrel was small enough to be concealed easily in her handbag or worn inconspicuously in a shoulder holster under a light jacket or cape. The other gun that she wore like an intimate article of clothing now lay on the bed in its small holster — a .22 two-shot derringer that she wore strapped to her right thigh.

As an operative for the Fenton Investigative Agency, Molly had been well trained in the use of firearms, but she had also been schooled in the art of jujitsu by a Japanese master. A lithe, athletic woman, she had learned to fight with her elbows and knees as well as her fists and feet. Her training had been complete when an ex-convict in New York taught her how to crack safes and pick locks.

While soaking in a tub of hot, soapy water, Molly thought ahead to her assignment in Creede. The case promised to be a routine one, more suited to a courier than an investigator, and Molly doubted that her skills would be put to use.

But then, she would have said the same thing about her trip to Cheyenne. In truth, even apparently routine cases were unpredictable, and by experience she had learned to be alert to danger anytime she became involved in the lives of people in trouble.

Her thoughts turned to Mrs. Boatwright and their ongoing disagreement. Molly knew she could never fully explain to the older woman why she had chosen this profession. Her work gave her a heightened appreciation of life, a sense of accomplishment that she had never known before and could not find in any other job open to her, a single woman. Molly was not willing to give that up for the staid, proper existence Mrs. Boatwright commended, and long ago she had decided she would not give it up until she found a man who could match the excitement and satisfaction of her profession.

III

At seven-twenty in the morning Molly left Union Station in the southbound passenger train. Seated in a thinly cushioned chair, she knew it would be one long, rump-sore day. But with a cloudless sky overhead she also knew the scenery would be spectacular. For that reason, she'd chosen a seat on the right side of the coach.

Both her expectations were fulfilled. Two hours later her rump was sore. But looking west out the coach window she saw a beautiful sight under a bright blue sky. Forested foothills, blue green with pines and spruce trees, shouldered against the rugged high peaks of the Rocky Mountains. Like peaks of whipped cream, the mountains were white with spring snows. Shortly before noon she saw the towering Pikes Peak high in the sky, the sentinel that had guided the earliest explorers and settlers.

Passengers on the train were the usual mixture of young and old, farmers and ranchers, townspeople and businessmen, and a few sleight-of-hand artists cruising the aisle. The gaunt man Molly had met on the train to Cheyenne was not among them. These shysters were territorial creatures, and his territory was probably north of Denver. Others had staked out this south-bound route.

After a stop in Colorado Springs, the train chugged on south to Pueblo and then headed for Walsenburg, pausing only for passengers and mail and to take on water. Long after nightfall Molly completed the first leg of her destination.

She stayed overnight in Walsenburg, and early the next morning boarded a Denver & Rio Grande westbound that took her into the mountains. This train was crowded with men, all eager to reach the silver mines.

Double-headed with two steam engines, the train crawled over Poncha Pass and roared into Alamosa with cinders rattling off the roof and bouncing against the windows. After a stop at the Alamosa station, the train angled into the San Juan Mountains, passing through Wagon Wheel Gap along the headwaters of the Rio Grande River. Soon the boomtown came into sight.

On the outskirts was a hodgepodge of rough cabins and lean-tos. Many residents, Molly noticed, were living in tents and wagons. Others, more prosperous, had built houses along Willow Creek, the tributary to the Rio Grande, and on a hill overlooking the town.

The unpainted frame-and-log buildings of Creede were jammed between the high vertical walls of Willow Creek Canyon and spilled out into an open meadow at the mouth. Bell ringing, the train nosed across this meadow and entered town one block off the main street, Creede Avenue.

The false-fronted and steep-roofed establishments of town were built within inches of one another, as though they were all trying to crowd closer to the mines in Willow Creek Canyon. The train slowed, the car couplings clanked as the engine stopped at the depot. The men clambered off the coach with duffel bags over their shoulders and battered suitcases in hand. They headed for Creede Avenue, the narrow street that led to the mines and mills in the canyon.

Carrying her valise, Molly followed the men. On Creede Avenue they were absorbed into the crowd that spilled off boardwalks and nearly filled the rutted street. Molly was amazed by the sight. From the barbershops and bathhouses to the many saloons and gambling houses every building and shack had the look of a stirred beehive.

At the corner of Wall Street and Creede

Avenue she saw the stock exchange, where shares of mining stock were bought and sold daily. A long line of men wearing crisply tailored suits and clean hats stretched out the door there, proof of the fact that stories of overnight wealth in "Colorado's treasure trove" had traveled with lightning speed across the country and even to Europe, and now investment money was pouring in.

With the reputable came the disreputable, and with the famous came the infamous. In the Denver papers Molly had read that Bat Masterson had opened the Denver Exchange, a saloon on this main street. Poker Alice dealt cards and chomped thick cigars in one of the clubs here. And Ford's Exchange was a gambling hall and saloon owned by Bob Ford, the man who had murdered Jesse James a decade ago in St. Joseph, Missouri.

The Orleans Club was not difficult to find. Near the far end of Creede, where the towering rock cliffs closed in, stood a large frame building with a mural-sized painting on its false front. The painting depicted scantily clad women skipping merrily through a meadow flowered with gold and silver coins. A sign in large black letters read: ORLEANS CLUB.

Molly stopped across the street from the

place. The din from within, a mixture of tinny piano music and raised voices, drifted through the batwing doors. Inside, Molly saw several young women among the crowd of men. She wondered if one of them was Sharon Hughes.

Molly turned away and backtracked through the crowd. She passed several other saloons, a drugstore and bookshop under one roof, a dress shop with dressed mannequins in the window, a bank called Merchants & Miners, and a row of three hotels among the reported one hundred in town, and then she followed a side street to the Fifth Avenue Hotel.

The Fifth Avenue Hotel, one block from Wall Street, was a two-story building of red brick. It was one of the most substantial structures in town, and as Molly came closer she saw that it was well guarded. A pair of uniformed men with sidearms stood at the double front doors, no doubt posted there to keep out the riffraff.

Molly smiled as she realized she did not qualify as riffraff. One of the guards tipped his cap to her while the other turned and opened the door.

She entered a high-ceilinged lobby where a large crystal chandelier cast sparkles of light and miniature rainbows down to the gleaming hardwood floor. Well-dressed men were seated in armchairs and settees, while others stood about in small groups, talking in subdued tones. Molly went to the desk, aware that several of them interrupted their business discussions long enough to gaze after her.

Her room reservation had been made in advance by telegraph, and after she checked in, a bellman carried her valise up a flight of stairs to the second floor. He took her to a suite midway down the hall, accepted a silver dollar with an extravagant bow, then departed, silently closing the door.

Molly undressed and lay on the bed for an hour and a half, recovering from two days of rocking passenger coaches and relentlessly clicking wheels. She got up then and dressed for the evening, slipping into a dark green dress. High-necked, it fit snugly over her breasts and waist and flared out at her hips. The dress was decorated with top stitching and a double row of pearl buttons down the front. Over her shoulders she wore a cape of matching material. The outfit was stylish, but functional, too. The cape effectively covered her shoulder holster.

After a prime-rib dinner in the dining room, Molly left the Fifth Avenue Hotel and followed the side street back to Creede Avenue. Evening light was rapidly fading, and just as quickly the air was growing cold. At an altitude of almost nine thousand feet the sun's warmth was soon missed.

The crowd on Creede's main street had scarcely diminished since Molly's arrival. As she made her way toward the walled canyon, she saw shadowy faces lighted by the glow of lamps from the windows of saloons and gambling halls. Most were bearded miners and mill workers, but others were clean-shaven men dressed in fine clothes. All were exuberant, looking for fortune and adventure at a gaming table or in an upstairs room.

From those rooms women beckoned. Molly heard their voices and looked up to see lighted windows where the prostitutes looked down upon the sea of men below. They called out their own names so a man would know who to ask for when he climbed a saloon's staircase and paid his money.

The canyon walls at the far end of Creede's business district made night shadows in the starry sky, and as Molly neared the Orleans Club she felt a cold breeze on her face. It wafted out of the canyon as though the door to an ice box had opened.

The Orleans Club was brightly lighted and crowded like the other establishments, but when Molly pushed through the batwing doors she saw that it was larger than it appeared from the street. The front section was a typical saloon, with a bar and brass footrail running the length of one wall, and bottles lining the backbar, where a pair of reclining nudes in a painting sleepily surveyed the scene.

The Orleans Club was halved by a partition, and a sign over the arched doorway back there read: THIS IS A SQUARE HOUSE. REPORT CHEATS TO PROPRIETOR.

"Hey, purty lady, you working upstairs?"

Molly saw that the question had been shouted by a squat man at the bar whose cheek bulged with a wad of tobacco. He must have been a miner who had just come off shift, for he still wore work clothes and boots spattered with mud.

Molly smiled as she walked by. "I don't work anywhere."

The miner's brow furrowed while he considered that, then he laughed loudly. He turned to his friends at the bar. "Hear that? She says —"

Molly moved on through the crowd, brushing shoulders and backs all the way to the doorway of the gambling hall. This parlor was quite different from the one she had seen in Cheyenne. Here the floor was bare planks with a scattering of sawdust instead of spittoons, and the tables and chairs were a hodgepodge collection, none matching. The dealers of faro and twenty-one were a rough-looking lot, men who openly wore guns — all but one, that is.

Molly moved through the sound and the smoke passing the smiling women at the elbows of the gambling men, to the back of the parlor. There she got a good look at the one female dealer here. She stood at a twenty-one table, sandy hair softly framing her down-turned face as she dealt cards with the unmistakable precision of a professional.

When Molly stepped closer to that table, the dealer lifted her gaze. Their eyes met, and then Molly saw the reddish birthmark high on her neck. She smiled, thinking that for once a father's boast had been true. Sharon was a very pretty young woman with large bright eyes and full lips above her firm chin.

Their gaze held for only a moment before Sharon turned her attention back to the game. But Molly sensed she had taken more than passing notice, probably wondering about this new woman in the Orleans Club. For the next half an hour Molly watched and listened to the good-natured conversation. Sharon was very popular with the men who played, even those who consistently lost.

"Care to try your luck, ma'am?"

Molly turned as a man moved beside her. He wore a full, dark beard that nearly covered his pockmarked face, and was dressed in a tailored suit and white shirt with ruffles down the front. Clenched between the fingers of one hand was a stubby cigar.

"I'll play at this table," Molly said, gesturing to Sharon, "when there's an opening."

"You know her?" he asked.

Molly shook her head.

"Other tables are open," he said, regarding her.

"I prefer to lose my money to another woman," Molly said with a smile.

"Sharon stays busy," he said. "Deals a good hand."

Molly had heard the tone of authority in his voice. "You're the manager of this club?"

"I'm Lou Drago," he said, his oiled hair gleaming in the lamplight. "I own the place. You are Miss . . . ?"

"Molly Owens," she replied.

"And you're here to gamble, right?" he asked.

"I enjoy the sport," Molly said. She added, "I've been known to win on occasion, but not often enough to form bad habits."

Drago's mouth curled into a smile. He

gave her a once-over, frankly appraising her physical attributes.

Molly realized that even though Creede was a wide-open camp, rarely if ever did a well-dressed woman enter a gambling parlor without an escort. Drago was curious about her, and probably a bit suspicious, too.

"I'll help you out," he said. "Get ready to buy some chips."

Molly watched as he shouldered his way through the knot of men at Sharon's table. They quickly stepped aside when they heard the owner's voice. Drago spoke into the ear of a man wearing a pinstriped suit. The man listened, replied with a quick nod, then picked up his chips and stepped back from the table. Drago motioned for Molly to take his place.

IV

As Molly stepped up to the table, she saw that Sharon Hughes had inherited her father's quick, friendly smile. Sharon greeted her, sold her fifty dollars' worth of chips, then shuffled and dealt the cards with a confident precision that she must have learned from her father.

Molly drew a pair of tens in the first hand and beat the dealer. Lou Drago, standing to one side, watched. Sharon shuffled again, but then loud shouts came from the saloon. Drago rushed away to see about the disturbance.

While Sharon dealt she carried on a light conversation with the men, calling them by name. When she came to Molly, she said, "New in Creede, aren't you?"

Molly nodded in reply, placing her bet of twenty dollars. Her down card was a king. She was showing a four.

"Staying long?" Sharon asked in a friendly tone.

Molly motioned for another card, knowing that there was more to Sharon's words than

41

friendly conversation. A moment of distraction could lead an amateur gambler into an error. "Not long," she replied, watching Sharon's hands. The next card off the deck was a seven.

Sharon finished dealing the hand. She turned up her down card, a nine. A four of spades and a six of diamonds were showing. "Beat nineteen, gents," she said, adding with a quick smile to Molly, "and lady."

Molly was the only player who topped the dealer without breaking twenty-one. The man at the end of the table commented that he had finally met Lady Luck, and other players chuckled in agreement.

"Staying in town just long enough to clean me out, is that it?" Sharon asked, smiling as she shuffled the cards.

Before Molly could reply, shouts erupted again in the saloon. The raised voice of Lou Drago was followed by the deep *boom* of a shotgun. The blast thundered through the room, creating immediate pandemonium.

Men tried to push their way toward the door while others tried just as hard to get away from it. Women shrieked. For a moment Molly thought everyone would panic into a human stampede. But then Drago shouted for quiet, and gradually the confusion and fear subsided.

Molly took advantage of this moment. She leaned across the twenty-one table and grasped Sharon's hand. "I must talk to you — privately."

Sharon drew back, suspicion clouding her face. "I don't know you."

"I know you don't," Molly said, "but you can trust me, Miss Hughes."

Surprise widened the young woman's eyes, then narrowed in anger. Molly had guessed that Sharon wasn't using her last name here.

"Who are you?" Sharon asked.

"My name is Molly Owens," she said. "I'm staying at the Fifth Avenue Hotel. Ask for me there tonight." Seeing doubt and suspicion in the young woman's expression, Molly squeezed her hand. "It's important, Sharon."

Molly released Sharon's hand and picked up the chips. She left the table and went to a cashier in a screened cage, where she cashed in her winnings. Then she left the gambling parlor.

"Excuse me, please . . . excuse me." At the sound of her voice, the men blocking the doorway moved aside, and Molly entered the saloon. Sprawled on the floor there was the body of a man who appeared to be a teamster. He wore a flannel shirt and denim trousers, and his wide-brimmed black felt hat lay on the floor a few feet away.

Lou Drago and three burly men who had the unmistakable look of bouncers stood nearby, encircled by the saloon crowd standing back a respectful distance. At first Molly thought the man had been killed by the shotgun, but now she saw the sawed-off weapon in the hands of an aproned bartender. Men at the bar were looking up, and Molly saw that the ceiling over the bar was speckled where rock salt had struck it.

As Molly moved around the edge of the crowd toward the door, she saw something else. A long-bladed knife lay beside the body where blood stained the plank floor. Evidently a fight had broken out and the teamster had been knifed, and to stop a murderous brawl Drago had ordered the bartender to fire off a load of rock salt.

Molly heard boots pounding on the boardwalk outside, and a moment later the batwing doors were punched open. A tall man wearing a Stetson came in. Molly glimpsed a city marshal's badge on his vest as he strode past her, and she got a close look at his face. He was distinctive, with a long jaw, light blue eyes, and a handlebar mustache. On his right hip in a low-slung holster was a Colt Peacemaker.

Onlookers were quickly gathering on the

boardwalk outside the Orleans Club. Leaving, Molly had to push her way through the morbidly curious, those eyes within bearded faces peering into the saloon.

Molly came out of the growing crowd and walked briskly past the darkened windows of the Windsor Bath House and the Herendeen Confectionery on her way back to the hotel. She wondered if Sharon's curiosity would outweigh her caution tonight.

Before going up to her room, Molly left word with the desk clerk of the Fifth Avenue Hotel that she expected a late-night visitor, a young woman, and that she should be allowed in.

Shortly after midnight Molly was dozing in a chair when she was roused by a light tapping on the door. She quickly got up and opened the door. Sharon stood in the hall, a tentative smile on her face.

"Lady, if you got rich enough at cards to stay in this place," she said, "you're a real inspiration to me."

Molly refrained from telling her that her own father was paying the bill, and answered with a smile, "Come in."

"I can't stay long," Sharon said, stepping through the doorway. "Lou thinks I'm on dinner break."

45

Molly closed the door. "You eat late in your line of work."

"I get off at four in the morning," Sharon said, looking around at the room's opulent furnishings. "I put in twelve hours, six days a week." She added with a note of pride, "Miners think they have it rough."

Sharon turned and faced Molly. "Let's get right to the point. You know my name. That means you know my father."

"Yes, I do —" Molly began.

"Well, I'm not going back to him," Sharon interrupted, "so if you're here to —"

Molly held out the roll of hundred-dollar bills, and Sharon abruptly fell silent. "Your father sent me here to give you this, Sharon. It's that simple."

Sharon's eyes had widened at the sight of the money, but now a look of suspicion came into her face. She made no move to take the money. "Just who are you, lady?"

Molly identified herself as a Fenton operative.

"So that's it," Sharon said. "Daddy hired a detective to hunt me down because he thinks he can soften me up with money —"

"No," Molly said firmly. "He understands how you feel. Believe me, he does." She went on to explain exactly why he wanted her to have the money, and concluded,

"There are no strings attached to it."

Sharon hesitated, then came a step closer and took the roll of greenbacks from Molly's hand. She quickly counted it, flipping back the corners with a gambler's expertise. She cast a hard look at Molly, but in the next moment her mouth quivered at the corners. Eyes blinking, large tears suddenly rolled down her cheeks, streaking her makeup.

Sharon covered her face with both hands. The bankroll came apart as it fell from her grasp, and greenbacks floated to the carpeted floor. Molly went to her and put an arm around her quaking shoulders. Sharon sobbed loudly.

Molly comforted her until her crying subsided. When Sharon took a deep breath and wiped her eyes with the palms of her hands, Molly saw the seventeen-year-old girl behind the rouge. The fast-talking, hard-edged woman was a facade that had been melted by tears. Or so Molly thought, until Sharon murmured something, her voice blurred with tears.

"What?" Molly asked softly.

Sharon cleared her throat. "My father's a fool, a damn fool."

"In what way?" Molly asked.

"Every way," Sharon said. She squared her shoulders and looked at Molly. "I know him too well, Miss Owens. He's a fool for women, and he's a fool for cards. He'll win a big pot one day and lose it all the next. I've seen it happen too many times. . . ." She looked down at the money scattered on the floor but made no move to pick it up. "One hundred dollars for every year of my life doesn't change that. It's nothing. . . ."

"Nothing?" Molly said.

"He seems to think seventeen hundred dollars is some kind of nest egg for me, doesn't he?" Sharon made a gesture of exasperation. "I have debts bigger than that. But daddy never owned anything in his life. He wouldn't know about investments."

Molly asked in surprise, "You're in debt?"

"Well, not exactly," Sharon replied. "I'm part owner of the Orleans Club. The owner, Lou Drago, sold stock in the club just like a mining company would sell shares in a mine. I was lucky enough to buy in, partly on credit. Now I'm working to pay for my partnership." She added, "So that's why seventeen hundred dollars doesn't look like much to me right now."

Molly wanted to ask how deeply in debt she was to Drago, but did not. "The money may not be a fortune, Sharon, but your father is giving it to you with the best of intentions."

"Oh, sure he is," Sharon said sarcastically, "just like all the other times he gave money to me. You know, that's about my only memory of him when I was growing up. Daddy was a smiling, handsome man with a beard who came to visit whatever relative I was living with. He'd hug me and talk to me for a few minutes, making vague promises for the future. Then he'd leave . . . after giving me some money." Her lip quivered.

Molly saw the pain of childhood memories in Sharon's eyes and realized she had developed a hard shell at a young age, a shell that kept her from being hurt.

As Molly knelt to help Sharon pick up the scattered money, she recalled the deep regret she had sensed in Dave Hughes. He was not a man to gloss over the past, and had confessed that he had not been a good father to his daughter. Now that Molly saw the depth of Sharon's anger toward him, she understood the sadness she had sensed in the man.

Molly went to the door with Sharon, hoping the girl would give her a message of some sort to relay to her father. But she did not.

Sharon opened the door and stepped out into the hall. She half-turned and paused as she looked back at Molly. Molly met her gaze and smiled.

"Good-bye, Miss Owens," Sharon said, briefly returning Molly's smile. Then she turned and hurried away.

Before leaving Creede on the morning passenger train, Molly went to the telegraph office in the depot and sent a full report to Dave Hughes. Then she sent a second wire to Horace Fenton in New York City, detailing the completion of her assignment.

Late the next day she arrived in Denver, wondering when her next assignment would come from the Fenton Investigative Agency. But as she arrived at Mrs. Boatwright's Boarding House for Ladies, she was met with a surprise. Waiting at the door was a clean-shaven man, battered hat in hand. His hair was cropped short, and he wore the khaki clothes of a laboring man, soiled green suspenders, and hobnailed boots. Her first impression was that he was here looking for work on the mansion grounds.

"I figured it's about time I did right by that girl," he said.

Molly stopped short, then moved a step closer, looking hard at him. He had a handsome face, the jaw was square with a strong chin, and in his gaze she saw the wild challenge of an eagle or hawk, a determination that she had not seen in him before.

"Dave," Molly whispered, scarcely believing the transformation. It had the effect of taking ten years off his appearance. "Dave Hughes."

"It's me," he said, grinning. "The day I got your report at the telegraph office, I gave up my table at the Stockmen's Inn and went straight to the barber. Then I traded clothes with the most surprised ditchdigger you ever saw."

Molly found herself at a loss for words. "I . . . I don't understand, Mr. Hughes."

"Like I said," he explained, "I figured it's about time I did right by that girl. I need your help. First, I want you to tell me everything that happened down there in Creede, and then I want you to —"

"Now hold on," Molly interrupted. "I'm no longer assigned to your case. I notified Mr. Fenton that I've completed the job."

"I figured as much," Hughes said, "and I fired off a message to Fenton. Told him I still need your services. He answered last night. Here." Reaching into the hip pocket of his soiled trousers, Hughes pulled out a folded sheet of paper. He handed it to her.

Molly unfolded it and saw that it came from the telegraph office in Cheyenne. The wire had originated in New York City.

Mr. Dave Hughes:

Rec'd your urgent message. Have in hand also a report from Operative Owens. The assignment has been fulfilled, and I understand you are satisfied with the job performed by her. I appreciate your concern for your daughter's safety, and you have my sincere sympathy in this heart-rending situation. However, due to the unique circumstances, Operative Owens is in a better position to decide whether or not she should accept this case than I am. Therefore, I shall leave it to her, and make no recommendation myself. If she wishes to continue the investigation under the terms you suggest, then she has my authorization to do so.

Am sending by telegraph a similar message to Operative Owens, and await her reply.

> Horace J. Fenton, President
> Fenton Investigative Agency
> New York City, New York

"Mr. Hughes," Molly said, "what is this about Sharon's safety? And exactly what is it you want me to investigate?"

"First, I want you to call me Dave," he said, "like you did a minute ago when you had that surprised look on your face." He grinned. "Okay if I call you Molly?"

She nodded.

"Now, Molly, like I said, I want to know everything that happened down there in Creede — and I mean everything. I know Sharon has low regard for me, so you don't need to spare anything on my account."

Molly studied his face, still surprised by the physical change in the man. "We'd better step inside."

Over a cup of steaming coffee from a silver decanter that a maid had brought into the front parlor of the mansion, Molly told Dave Hughes of her meeting with Sharon. She did as she was asked, sparing few details. While she spoke, she saw the man's face tighten, and by the time she finished he had a faraway look as he stared fixedly at the floor. He did not speak for a long time.

All the while Molly was aware of Mrs. Boatwright's lingering presence. The landlady passed by the doorway several times as she examined this gentleman caller, and Molly caught more than one severe look from her.

"Well, Sharon's got every right to feel that

way," Dave said at last. "I reckon about the only thing she ever learned from me was how to deal cards." He paused. "But that doesn't mean I'm going to sit back here and do nothing while Lou Drago bleeds her white."

"You know Drago?" Molly asked.

"I know him by reputation," Dave replied. "And I know some gamblers who've worked for him. He's a bad one."

"What do you mean?" Molly asked.

"I'll tell you what his game is," Dave said, "in case you haven't figured it out for yourself. Drago's financing that Orleans Club on the backs of his employees. They'll never see a return on their so-called investment. That's because Drago will keep draining the profit into his own pocket, leaving Sharon and the other investors waiting for a payday that will never come. They'll always be in debt to Drago, and in the end they'll be left holding some worthless pieces of paper he calls stock certificates."

"You can prove that?" Molly asked.

"No," he replied, "but my nose tells me Drago is running a confidence game." He paused. "But that isn't the worst of it."

"What do you mean?" Molly asked.

"Drago is a ruthless man," Dave said. "I know he's ordered dealers beaten who were suspected of skimming. Suspected, mind you. Fingers broken, faces smashed up, you name it — Drago has a way of making a point."

"If you know all this," Molly said, "then you should take the evidence to the U.S. marshal's office."

Dave shook his head. "The gamblers who have told me about Lou Drago would never testify. Call it a code of honor in the profession, or whatever you want, but those men would rather limp on to the next boomtown than take a witness chair." He leaned toward Molly. "But I know it's true. The man's ruthless — and he has my daughter."

"What do you want me to do?" Molly asked.

"Two things," Dave replied. "I want you to find out everything you can about Drago. The more we get on him, the better. Then I want you to lay everything out to Sharon. Tell her exactly what she's gotten herself into."

"Think she'll listen to me?" Molly asked.

"I hope so," Dave replied. "She sure as hell won't listen to what I have to say. At least she won't slam the door in your face." He added, "Molly, you've got to try. You're my only hope."

"But if I convince her that Drago has

robbed her," Molly said, "she might do something foolish. And if Drago is the desperate man you say he is . . ." Molly did not need to finish the thought to make her point.

"I've thought of that," Dave said. "We'll both be there, and we'll have to protect her somehow."

Molly shook her head skeptically.

"Do this much for me," Dave said. "Investigate Drago's background. Give me as much information on him as you can dig up."

"Then what?" Molly asked.

"Then you can decide whether or not you want to pursue this any further," he replied. "It'll be up to you, pure and simple."

Nothing in this business is ever simple, Molly thought, and with Dave Hughes everything seemed to turn out to be more complicated than it first appeared.

At last she said, "All right, I'll do a background check on Lou Drago."

Dave grinned. "Good!" He stood.

"But I must warn you," Molly said, "there's a good chance I won't be able to take this case, a very good chance."

"Sure, I understand," Dave said, moving toward the entryway that led to the front hall.

Molly followed him. "Where are you going?"

"To Creede," he replied over his shoulder.

"Bring your report to me down there."

"But where will you be?" Molly asked, hurrying after him.

Dave had reached the front door. He pulled it open and looked back at her. "Don't worry, I'll find you. So long."

"But, Dave —" Molly began. She watched helplessly as he left the mansion, pulling the door shut after him.

Molly slapped her hands together. Turning around, she saw Mrs. Boatwright standing in the hall. Arms folded under her ample breasts, the landlady looked sternly at her.

"I don't understand you, Molly Owens," she said. "I swear I don't. Beautiful and intelligent as you are, you'll run after a man like that. Molly, he wasn't even *clean*."

Molly heard her speak that last word with great distaste, the severest indictment of all. "It's not what you think," she said, and headed for the staircase.

"I've got eyes," Mrs. Boatwright said with an air of finality.

In no mood for a reprimand, even a motherly one, Molly replied more sharply than she intended, "One day I'll tell you what you just saw."

Mrs. Boatwright thrust out her pink hand. In her grasp was an envelope. "Came for you," she said huffily.

Molly recognized the envelope from the telegraph office at Denver's Union Station. She took it from Mrs. Boatwright's outstretched hand. The landlady turned away without a word and strode heavily down the hall.

Molly tore open the envelope and quickly read the message inside. As she expected, it was from Horace Fenton, telling her to use her best judgment in deciding whether to stay on the Hughes case, and to report back as soon as possible. She'd already made her decision, she thought, for better or worse.

In the morning Molly began her investigation at the U.S. marshal's office. The bespectacled clerk in the documents room knew her, and took only a few minutes to find the file marked LOUIS R. DRAGO. It was a fat one.

Drago himself had never been placed under arrest by either federal or local lawmen, but he was no stranger to them. Molly scanned dozens of disturbance and arrest reports from saloons and brothels that listed him as owner or a partner in ownership of the establishments. The bail for those employees arrested was often put up by Drago. One report even referred to him as the "kingpin of Denver's criminal element."

However, no warrants for his arrest were outstanding.

Molly took notes from these reports, then returned the file to the clerk. On a whim she asked if there was a file on a gambler named Dave Hughes. The clerk made a search through the oak file cabinets and came back shaking his head. Hughes had committed no crimes in Colorado and wasn't wanted for any federal crime in any state.

Feeling a bit guilty for her suspicion, she started to leave. But when her name was spoken, she turned and saw a round-faced man coming out of an office. He was pear-shaped, and looked nothing like a lawman, but on the vest of his three-piece suit was pinned the brass badge of a federal marshal.

"Miss Owens?" he said. "May I speak to you a moment?"

Molly backtracked and followed him into his office. Scarcely more than a cubbyhole, the space was taken up by an old, flattopped desk and two chairs. He motioned to one of them as he moved behind the desk and lowered himself into a creaking swivel chair.

"I'm Philips, Saul Philips," he said. "I understand you're a Fenton operative."

Molly nodded. "That's right."

"You're on the trail of Lou Drago?" he asked.

"I'm not exactly on his trail," Molly said. "I know where he is."

"In Creede," Philips said.

Molly nodded again. She watched as Philips regarded her, aware that beneath his formal politeness was an ingrained mistrust of private investigative agencies and their operatives. Molly had earned the respect of the officer in charge of the Denver office, but she had never met Philips.

"I overheard you request the file on Drago," he went on. "I don't normally aid private investigators, but in this case I'm inclined to make an exception. I thought that if you hadn't yet tracked Drago down, I could tell you where to find him."

"I appreciate the offer," Molly said.

He nodded slowly, still studying her. "Few women are in your business, and I must say you don't look the part."

Molly resisted the temptation to say the same thing about him. From his physique and soft hands, Molly could see that he was not the sort of lawman who spent countless days in the saddle and nights under the stars in search of outlaws.

"I'll take that as a compliment," she said. Philips seemed to be a humorless man, but that remark brought a brief smile to his fleshy face.

"May I ask what your interest is in Lou Drago?" he asked.

Molly shook her head. "It's confidential."

"I thought you'd say that," he said mildly.

"May I ask you what the law's interest is in him?" Molly asked.

The swivel armchair creaked again under his weight when he leaned back. His chin disappeared into folds of flesh as he gazed down at his cluttered desk top, obviously debating whether to answer. He was not obligated to do anything more than supply written records to her or to any other citizen.

"I don't wish Drago any good fortune, Miss Owens," Philips said at last. After another long pause the big lawman came down in the chair, hard, his small eyes fixed on Molly. "I had him all but nailed on a murder, but he slipped through my fingers."

"If you know where he is —" Molly began.

"Miss Owens," he interrupted, "locating the bastard . . . uh, pardon me . . . locating Drago is not the problem. Finding my witness murdered on Market Street was the problem."

"I see," Molly said. The intensity of Philips's anger caught her by surprise. He appeared to have all the emotions of a potato, until he slammed down in his chair.

Recalling the Drago case brought a snarl to his mouth and passion to his voice.

"I've been in law enforcement a long time, Miss Owens," he said, "and like anybody else in this business I've seen some horrible sights. But the one I can't get over is the brutal murder of that woman. I won't tell you how my witness died. Suffice it to say that she suffered a long time before it was over."

"Drago did it?" Molly asked.

"Obviously I don't have the evidence to bring him into court," Philips said, "or he wouldn't be a free man right now, building his little empire down there in Creede." He waved a fat hand at her. "But I have no doubt he murdered that young woman — or ordered the job done. Drago wasn't only silencing a witness, he was sending out a clear message to anyone else who might consider testifying against him."

Molly remembered that Dave Hughes had made nearly the same observation about Lou Drago. "Seems strange that in all of his scrapes with the law, he's never been charged with a crime, much less arrested."

"Strange," Philips replied with a tone of irony.

Molly met his steady gaze. "Drago has a local politician or two on his payroll?"

"Such allegations have been made," Philips replied noncommittally.

"Are they true?" Molly asked.

"Unproven," he said.

"But true," Molly persisted.

"As a matter of legality," Philips said, "I can't comment further."

"You don't have to," Molly said, smiling. She asked, "Is there anything else you can tell me about Drago?"

Phillips shook his head slowly.

Molly stood. "Well, I'm glad we talked. You've been very helpful."

"Are you going after Drago?" he asked, looking up at her.

She smiled again. "I can't comment on that."

Saul Phillips smiled, despite himself. "You don't have to," he said. "But you can do one thing for me."

"What?" Molly asked.

"If you get anything on Lou Drago," he said, "let me know. I'm not a free-lancer like you, so I can't go after him until I have a reason — a reason I can take into a courtroom."

"Fair enough," Molly said. "If I should happen to stumble across a piece of evidence, I'll see that you're the first to know." She turned to leave.

"One more thing, Miss Owens," Phillips said.

She turned back and looked at the pear-shaped lawman sitting behind his desk like an enormous toad.

"Be careful around Lou Drago," he said in a flat, humorless tone. "Be damned careful."

VI

Three days after her meeting with Marshal Saul Philips, Molly arrived by train in Creede. She found the mountain mining camp as busy as it was when she had left nearly a week ago. Men were jammed shoulder to shoulder on the boardwalks and streets, and even more were crowded into the business and sporting establishments, those weathered structures that could have tumbled out of Willow Creek Canyon like so many giant blocks.

Molly went straight to the Fifth Avenue Hotel on Wall Street. This time she took a corner room. Luxuriously furnished with a walnut writing desk, easy chair, and a dresser with matching nightstand, the room featured a gleaming black marble fireplace and a thick wool carpet. The room's one window looked out over the street toward the busy intersection at Creede Avenue. Upon checking in, Molly had ordered a bath. After undressing, she washed cinders and soot out of her long blond hair. Then she sank into a tub of steaming soapy water for a long soak.

Now as she stretched out on the bed she

thought about the case and the investigation that lay ahead, and into her mind came Philips's word of warning. The potential for violence was much greater than she had first realized, and as she thought about the personalities involved, she had the sensation of watching a fuse burn toward a powder keg. Sharon Hughes was a strong-minded young woman who was determined to make her own way in life, and her father was just as determined to "rescue" her from Lou Drago. Then there was Drago himself. . . .

Molly's thoughts were interrupted by a knock on the door. She got up and quickly put on a robe, and wrapped her wet hair in a towel, turban style. The knock came again, louder.

"Who is it?" Molly asked. When no answer came, she went to her handbag and pulled out the .38. Moving to the door, she eased it open.

"Told you I'd find you," Dave Hughes said, flashing his grin.

"You could have given me some warning," Molly said.

His smile faded. "I guess I should have. But as soon as I found out you were registered, I came running."

Molly noted that he was dressed in the same work clothes she had seen him wearing in Denver. "I'm surprised you were let in the front door."

"Took some fancy talking on my part," he replied, "but once I convinced the guards and the desk clerk that you were my long-lost sister, they let me in."

Molly smiled, shaking her head. *Clothes don't make the man,* she thought. No matter how Dave Hughes looked, he could talk his way into any private club or hotel.

"I shouldn't have barged in like this," he said, backing away a step. "We can talk later."

"No," Molly said. "As long as you're here, come in and I'll give you my report — if you can stand the sight of me."

He grinned. "You look beautiful . . . sis." He laughed and walked into the room, heading for the easy chair.

Molly repeated everything Saul Philips had told her, then referred to her notes as she related the contents of the Drago file in the documents room of the U.S. marshal's office. The gambler listened, his face lined with a grim expression.

"I was hoping there was a warrant out for Drago," Dave said when she finished.

"If there were," Molly said, "you can be sure Philips would have him behind bars, if not on a gallows with a hangman's noose around his neck."

Dave thought for a moment. "I wonder if there's some way we could turn Philips loose on him. Maybe we can concoct a crime and pin it on Drago —"

"I don't work that way, Dave," Molly interrupted.

He looked at her. "Ethics?"

"Something like that," Molly said.

"Ethics mean nothing to a mad dog," Dave said.

"Is that what you think Drago is?" she asked.

"From the information you've gathered," Dave replied, "I'd say he qualifies."

"Then let's prove it," Molly said, "and put him away."

Dave grinned. "That means you'll take the case."

Too late, Molly realized that she had stepped into his verbal trap. "I know one thing," she said. "Sharon deserves to know the truth about Drago's background."

"You'll tell her?" he asked.

Molly met his gaze and saw an eagerness there that was almost boyish. For all the cool and detached manner he showed at the poker table, he was a man filled with hopes and uncertainties. Molly replied with a nod.

"Good!" he exclaimed, leaping to his feet. "She'll listen to you. I know she will." He moved rapidly to the door. "Then we'll get my girl out of here."

Molly didn't say so, but she had her doubts about that.

Her wake-up call came as a loud rapping on her door at three-thirty in the morning. She opened her eyes to the cold and silent darkness of the early hour, a time that made her think of a tomb.

After lighting a lamp, she splashed cold water on her face, combed out her hair, and pinned it up. Twenty minutes later she left the room, a shoulder holster concealed under her light jacket, and walked out of the hotel. The desk clerk watched her with a cocked eyebrow.

The scene on Creede Avenue at this hour was eerie, and she felt as though she had somehow passed through starry darkness in the San Juan Mountains and entered another planet. The pale glow of kerosene lamps in saloons and gambling halls cast light across the boardwalks and into the empty street, making strange, elongated shadows.

In the night silence a few men made their way from one saloon to another, swaying drunkenly as they tried to focus on the next pair of batwing doors. At this hour upright pianos were still, no brass bands blared, and the upstairs windows where the painted women had beckoned passersby were dark. All that remained now, Molly saw as she walked along the boardwalk with the hollow sounds of her heels tapping on the planks, were the devout gamblers, ever sober, who played their games of chance with quiet intensity as though in prayer.

Molly entered the Orleans Club. The saloon was quiet and darkened except for a single lamp on the bar where a swamper mopped the floor by the brass footrail. Behind the bar an aproned bartender was cleaning glasses, a dead cigar clenched between his teeth. He looked up at the sound of the swinging doors and regarded Molly as she crossed the room to the gambling parlor.

The only players left were the half-dozen clustered around the twenty-one table at the far end of the room. All the other dealers had closed and now were counting the take under the watchful eyes of three burly men armed with sawed-off shotguns. As Molly crossed the room she heard a feminine voice announce that the table was closed. The players drifted away, heading for the door. Sharon had dealt her last hand for the night.

"I can see who the most popular dealer in the Orleans Club is," Molly said as she reached the table.

Sharon looked up and surprise registered on her face, but she did not smile.

Molly said, "Can we talk?"

Sharon cast a nervous glance at the other dealers, who were counting money as the armed men looked on. "Not now. You . . . you'll have to leave while I finish up."

"All right," Molly said. "I'll be waiting for you outside by the front door."

Sharon nodded curtly.

Molly turned, crossed the gambling parlor, and left the Orleans Club through the saloon. The bartender shut the door behind her. In twenty minutes the house dealers straggled out, walking silently into the darkness as they went their separate ways. Molly stood on the boardwalk while the minutes dragged past.

The night silence was broken by the squeal of rusty door hinges. The sound came from somewhere behind the club, but several moments passed before Molly realized the significance of it. She rushed up the boardwalk to the corner of the building and hurried through the pitch-black passageway between the Orleans Club and the hotel next door.

Reaching the back alley, Molly looked one way and then the other. By pale starlight she saw a huddled figure striding toward the night shadows of Willow Creek Canyon. Molly followed.

The alley joined Creede Avenue where it entered the canyon. Here the sheer stone walls narrowed around the gurgling creek, scarcely leaving room for the road and the narrow-gauge railroad tracks in the canyon bottom.

The high canyon walls blocked out most of the starlight, and Molly lost sight of the figure ahead. She walked on at a measured pace, hoping she wouldn't overtake Sharon and that the noise of the creek would cover the sounds of her footfalls.

A quarter of a mile farther the canyon widened. Molly saw the rectangular shapes of buildings looming in the near-darkness. A line of squat cabins, boardinghouses, and stores was ahead, all with black windows.

Molly realized this was Upper Creede, the original settlement that had sprung up around the first silver strike in 1889. As mineral discoveries increased over the next two years, the town needed room and had expanded into the meadow at the mouth of the canyon. Now ten thousand people lived there, and the booming camp had become the county seat.

Molly slowed her pace when she saw a faint glow of light ahead. She angled off the road toward it, passing a long, two-story boardinghouse. Golden lamplight filtered out a window of a small log cabin built against the stone cliff.

Molly moved through high grass and weeds to the window. Inside, it was covered by a gauze curtain. She bent down and peered through a gap at the bottom. Sharon was inside, buttoning up the front of an ankle-length flannel nightgown.

The flame in the oil lamp was turned low, but in the moments before Sharon blew out the lamp Molly saw the bare furnishings in the cabin — a rickety table with two battered chairs, a counter of rough pine, an empty powder box nailed to the wall for a cupboard, and a rug of braided rags at the foot of an iron bed. In a corner of the room stood a pair of mud-caked boots, and from a nail in the log wall above them hung a work shirt and a pair of denim trousers, muddy too.

Molly backed away from the window the moment after Sharon blew out the lamp and crawled into bed. A man was sleeping there.

Molly returned to the Fifth Avenue Hotel, hunching her shoulders against the cold breeze that swept down Willow Creek Canyon. At the mouth of the canyon the breeze hissed through boughs of pine trees like whispered secrets. Back in her hotel room, Molly undressed and blew out the lamp, but she didn't go to bed.

She sat in the chair, staring into the darkness of the elegantly furnished room. Her thoughts were as dark and cold as the night. In her profession she slipped into the lives of others, into their hopes, their dreams, their fears. Inevitably she became a part of their aspirations, sometimes an obstacle, but more often a threat. At best she was regarded as an intruder; at worst, a spy.

Tonight she had felt like a spy. Now she knew Sharon had kept at least one secret from her father — an important one. Were there others? Probably.

In a way, Molly didn't want to find out. This young woman had a right to live life on her own terms, and a right to suffer the consequences. Molly didn't want to invade Sharon's privacy. Yet, she knew she would.

Molly awoke long after sunup, hearing street sounds of passing wagons and the shouts of men. Sitting up in bed, she realized she had been awakened by the exuberant calls and curses of bull whackers and the loud popping of whips. Bull trains and mule trains were used to haul goods and equipment to mines beyond the railhead, and to bring ore down from them to the mills in Willow Creek Canyon.

After breakfast Molly saw some of these teamsters at work as she retraced her steps to Upper Creede. The men were a flamboyant lot who tipped their floppy-brimmed hats to her in extravagant gestures while calling out morning greetings. In the next moment they turned to curse their animals or the engineer of a passing steam engine who blew the shrill whistle to frighten the harnessed animals.

Molly watched with amusement. From experience she knew that railroaders and teamsters did not get along as a rule, and miners did not take to either group. In other camps she had seen these clannish men stake out their saloons, and rarely were the lines crossed. A railroader in a teamster saloon wanted trouble.

Molly walked to Upper Creede, seeing the buildings in the canyon bottom by daylight now. She recognized the long boardinghouse beside the road. Next door, almost hidden, stood the log cabin that backed against the canyon wall.

Molly followed a well-worn footpath to the cabin. The door was made of warped planks that had weathered to a light gray color. She rapped on it.

After waiting half a minute she knocked again. She heard muffled sounds inside, probably a pair of bare feet hitting the floor from the bed. Presently the door opened a crack.

The instant Molly's eyes met Sharon's, the door slammed shut. From inside Molly heard an exasperated curse.

"Sharon," Molly said through the door, "you can talk to me now, or tonight at the Orleans Club."

The door slowly opened. Sharon looked out, her youthful face puffed with sleep. She glared at Molly.

"What does my father want now?" she demanded. "I thought you said he gave me that money with no strings attached."

"He did," Molly said.

"Then why won't you leave me alone?" she asked.

"After you've listened to what I have to say, I will," Molly said. "That is, if you still want me to."

Sharon blinked. "What's this about?"

"I'd like to come in," Molly said, "and tell you."

She hesitated, then nodded. "All right." She opened the door all the way and stepped back.

Molly entered the cabin and saw that the man who had slept there last night was gone. The pillows on the rumpled bed showed the imprint of two heads.

Sharon led her to the table at the kitchen end of the one-room cabin and pulled out a chair. Crossing the room, Molly felt heat radiating from the soot-blackened iron stove. She sat down in the chair Sharon offered.

Molly smiled at her. "You're married now?"

Sharon's eyes widened with amazement at the remark.

Molly gestured to the stove. "I suppose you get up and fix breakfast for your husband, and after he leaves to start his shift, you go back to bed."

"You've been following me," Sharon said,

anger rising in her voice. "Just what the hell do you want?"

Molly said, "You were right about your father sending me here. He wants me to explain a bad situation to you."

"What situation?" she asked.

"Lou Drago and the Orleans Club," Molly said.

"Lou?" Sharon said. "What about him?"

"I interviewed a U.S. marshal in Denver and learned some things you should know," Molly said. She went on to relate her conversation with Saul Philips, then repeated Dave's theory about Drago's sale of stock certificates in the Orleans Club. By the time she finished, Sharon's mouth was set and she was glowering at Molly.

"Your father's concerned about you," Molly said, "and I think he has good reason to —"

"Daddy doesn't even know him," Sharon interrupted, her voice thick with emotion. "Lou's a good man. Go back to Cheyenne and tell daddy that. And tell him once and for all to leave me alone. I don't know why that's so hard for him to do now after all those years when he didn't want me." The corners of her mouth quivered as she fought to control her emotions.

"Would you talk to him if you had the

79

chance?" Molly asked.

"No!" Sharon snapped. "That isn't possible. I have my own life here. . . ." Her voice trailed off.

"Perhaps I can make it possible," Molly said.

"No," Sharon said again. She looked at Molly suddenly. "And don't you get any ideas about bringing him here!"

"Sharon —" Molly began.

She stood. "I think you'd better go."

Molly looked up at her, again aware that Sharon was a girl and a woman in the same body. The girl was angry at her father, and the woman was eager to be independent.

"Please go," Sharon said.

Molly followed the wagon road back to town. She went to the Mineral County Courthouse, a simple frame building near the mouth of Willow Creek Canyon. A clerk there pulled out a large volume marked RECORDS, and Molly went through all the pages for the last eight months. No marriage license had been issued in the name of Sharon Hughes or to any other woman with that first name.

Leaving the courthouse, Molly made her way down the crowded boardwalk on Creede Avenue. Amid the sea of men's faces and bobbing hats of all descriptions, she missed the one that was familiar.

Dave swept up beside her and took her arm. Without a word he guided her to a recessed doorway under a sign lettered in elaborate script: OLDS BROS. CAFÉ HOME COOKING.

"I was sitting in the Denver Exchange with a handful of bad cards," he said, "and I looked out the window and saw you, the prettiest woman in this town."

"You've seen them all?" Molly asked.

"I'm working on it," Dave replied with a laugh. "Let's go in here."

There was a disturbance inside the Olds Bros. Café. A loud-voiced man, clearly drunk, was shouting at a cook wearing a white apron. The pair stood near the kitchen doorway, arguing, while several miners and townsmen looked on.

"You don't have to eat that beef stew," the cook was saying, "and you don't have to pay. All you have to do is get out."

"I'm not through with you yet," the drunk said, swaying on his feet. He was a stout man with a shrill voice. "You tried to poison me with this tripe. That sign outside says 'home cooking,' and I should have known —"

"Get out," the cook said, his jaw jutting. "I've heard enough out of you."

"Let me finish," the drunk said loudly. "I should have taken that sign as a warning, shouldn't I? Hell, if I wanted home cooking, I would've stayed home. I didn't come to Creede to get rich. I came here to get away from ma's cooking."

Several of the men watching laughed.

Encouraged, the drunk turned to them. "Home cooking where I come from will kill you. Ma could burn water. She could touch a ladle to cream and curdle it. Home cooking! Hell, no, I don't want none of that. I want good restaurant cooking, served up by a pretty girl. Any girl who don't look like my sister is pretty. Ma can't cook, and sis can't look. Now, I've got an aunt who can wither a daisy with one glance. And, by God, you ought to see *her* daughter —"

The cook had gone into the kitchen and now he came back with a flour-covered rolling pin. He raised it over the drunk's head and swiftly brought it down, stopping him in midsentence.

Molly saw the stout man crumple to the floor. While the onlookers watched, the cook dragged him out of the café through the back door to the alley.

"Now, you folks sit yourselves down," the cook said after he closed the back door and came through the kitchen. "We serve good food here, nothing but the best."

"Uh, just coffee," Dave said to him. "Two cups of coffee here." He sat with Molly at a table near the window that opened out to the crowded boardwalk. Dave glanced back toward the kitchen where the onlookers had returned to their seats. "Sometimes I think the world is going crazy," he said in a low voice.

"Or already has," Molly said.

Dave studied her. "Did you see Sharon last night?"

Molly nodded. "And this morning."

"What happened?" he asked.

Molly recounted her two meetings with Sharon. By the time she finished, Dave's shoulders were slumped and he stared vacantly at the cup of black coffee before him.

"Did she come to Creede by herself," Molly asked, "or with a man?"

Dave shook his head. "I don't think she knew any men in Cheyenne — not that way." He paused. "They aren't married?"

"Not in Mineral County," Molly said.

"Well," Dave said, exhaling, "I reckon that's something else she learned from me, that, and dealing cards."

Molly asked a question that had been on her mind for some time: "Any idea how much money Sharon had when she first came to Creede?"

"I don't how much she had saved up on her own," he replied, "but I know I came home that night she left with three hundred and forty dollars in my wallet."

Molly caught the implication. It was a secret only a father would keep.

"And I reckon most of it went straight into Lou Drago's pocket," Dave went on, "along with that seventeen hundred." He slapped a hand down on the table top. "Hell, I don't care about the money she took from me. What I care about is that she's hooked up with Lou Drago. The bastard's picked her clean, and she doesn't even know it."

"Sharon's determined to make her own way in life," Molly said.

"I know, I know," Dave said. "And I'd be willing to leave matters right there if it wasn't for Drago. Damn!" His fist clenched on the table before him.

"What do you plan to do now?" Molly asked.

"Exactly what I came here to do," Dave replied. "I'm going to bust Drago's operation."

"You came here to help your daughter," Molly reminded him.

Dave conceded the point with a nod. "Now it looks like the best way to help

Sharon is to run Drago out of this camp."
He paused. "And I'm going to need your
help to do the job."

Molly shook her head.

"You'll just go off and leave Sharon in this
fix?" he asked.

"What you're asking me to do is out of my
line of work," Molly said.

"What do you mean?" he asked.

"I'm an investigator," she said, "not a vig-
ilante."

"I'm not asking you to do anything illegal," Dave protested. "All I'm asking is
that you continue your investigation. Find
out all you can about Lou Drago, who his
associates are — everything with his name
on it."

Molly considered that. "If I turn up any
evidence that he's committed a crime, I'll
turn it over to the law. You know that, don't
you?"

"Oh, sure," Dave said. "Ethics, right?"

"I meant it when I told you I'm not a vigi-
lante," Molly said, unsmiling. "I won't aid
anyone who intends to take the law into his
own hands."

"That's how you've got me figured?" he
asked.

"I don't have you figured," Molly replied.
"I think you have some hidden agendas.

85

That's why I'm telling you where I stand."

"Fair enough," Dave said. "Then you'll take the case?"

"I'll finish what I started with the Drago investigation," Molly said. "On one condition."

"Condition," he repeated. "What condition?"

"That you tell me what you're doing," Molly replied. "At all times."

"That's easy enough," Dave said. "I'll be playing cards with all the other amateurs around here. I've got to have some money to pay your expenses, don't I?" He added, "Don't worry, I'll stay out of your way. And I'll stay clear of Sharon, too. No point in letting her know I'm in town."

Molly nodded in agreement. "How will I contact you?"

"I'll find you," he said.

Molly shook her head. "That isn't a good idea."

"It'll have to do," Dave said. "Look, if I'm going to act the part of a fumbling card-player who gets lucky once in a while, I can't make many plans. I can't say ahead of time where I'll be, or when I can pull out of a game. See what I mean?"

"All right," Molly said reluctantly. "We'll do this your way."

"Good," Dave said. He picked up his hat and stood. "I'll check in with you from time to time . . . sis." Without giving her a chance to reply, he turned and went out the door.

Molly watched him leave. She had been close to resigning from this case. She felt certain that Dave had more up his sleeve than a few aces. But he had been right about one thing. She could not go off and leave Sharon at this point.

Molly left the Olds Bros. Café and joined the river of humanity that flooded the boardwalk and spilled out into the rutted street. The more she thought about this arrangement with Dave Hughes, the less she liked it. In her method of working she was accustomed to gathering information and then making periodic reports to her clients. Dave insisted on reversing the procedure by coming to her for reports on the investigation. As a paying client, he had a right to do that, but still Molly felt uncomfortable with the idea. There was enough unpredictability in her business without adding more.

But from the beginning this case had been unconventional, and now Molly realized that much of Dave's life had been that way. Since the death of his wife he had lived by his wits, drifting from one gambling hall to another until he'd landed steady work at the Stockmen's Inn. That was when he made the decision to settle down and give his daughter a home, determined to be the father that he had not been over the past decade and a half.

Too late, Molly thought; *too much lost time.* She was swept along with the crowd on the boardwalk, thinking that she could not help Dave recapture the past. But she sympathized with him, and knew that he shouldered the guilt for Sharon's involvement with Lou Drago. If anything happened to her because of it, Dave would feel responsible.

Pushing and cajoling her way out to the edge of the boardwalk, Molly crossed the street at an angle that took her to the batwing doors of the Orleans Club. She entered and was surprised to see that the saloon was nearly full at this hour of the morning.

She felt the stares of men as she crossed the saloon to the arched doorway of the gambling parlor. A quick look into that room, half-empty, confirmed her guess that Sharon was not yet on duty.

But Drago was not there either. Wondering if he had an office in the back, she turned and moved toward the lines of men standing three and four deep at the bar. The bartender saw her coming and stepped toward that end of the bar, a look of curiosity wrinkling his brow.

"Ma'am?" he said, peering over the shoulders of two men who appeared to be mill workers.

"I'm looking for Mr. Drago," Molly said. "Is he here?"

"No, ma'am," the bartender replied. "You might find him in his office. He generally goes there first thing of a mornin'."

"Where is that?" Molly asked.

"Just down the street a couple blocks," he replied, motioning out to Creede Avenue with a sweep of his arm. "Look for the San Juan Building on the corner."

Outside, a train of cars loaded with ore concentrate steamed out of Willow Creek Canyon, and the bright sky was briefly darkened by the engine's plume of black smoke. Molly followed the boardwalk two blocks down the street. At the corner there she looked up at the large building where a sign over the double doors read: SAN JUAN BLDG.

She had noticed this building the day she had first climbed off the passenger train at the depot. It was one of the more elaborate structures in town, with decorative trim at the windows and a rounded cupola on the peak of its steep roof. Across the street was the stock exchange.

The front doors opened into a foyer. On the wall was an office directory. Molly read down the list of names and saw that investment companies and several attorneys and accountants had offices here. Among the names was Louis R. Drago, in room 215.

Molly moved down the hall to a staircase and climbed the steps to the second floor. Brass numbers were on the doors and midway down the hall she found 215. She knocked on it.

The masculine voice that answered was vaguely familiar, and when Molly opened the door she found that it belonged to Drago. He sat behind a massive desk, a thick cigar in his mouth, his black eyebrows arched as he looked at her in mild surprise.

"Mr. Drago?" Molly asked.

"Yeah," he said, taking the cigar from his mouth. He gazed at her and then half-stood, beckoning with the cigar. "Come in, come in."

Molly closed the door and moved toward him. Drago kept an orderly desk with a neat stack of papers under a cut-glass paperweight, a pen and bottle of ink in the center, and a wooden humidor to one side.

"My name is Molly Owens —"

"Yeah, wait a minute," he said, jabbing the cigar in the air like a professor might use a pointer. "I know you from somewhere, don't I? Denver?" He squinted as he thought. "No, wait a minute, right here in Creede. You've been in my club, right?"

"Yes, I —"

"Yeah, I recollect," he said. "You play twenty-one, right?"

"On occasion, I do," Molly said.

"Uh-huh, I recollect," Drago said, returning the cigar to his mouth with a self-satisfied look. "Can't remember if you won or not. I run a square house. If you lost and you're here to —"

This time Molly interrupted him. "I didn't lose, Mr. Drago."

"That's good, that's good," he said. "Everybody wins. That's good." He paused, eyes narrowing. "Then what're you here for?"

"May I sit down?" Molly asked.

"Yeah, sure," he said, snatching the cigar from his mouth. "I shoulda offered . . . here, take this chair."

Molly moved to the side of the big desk and sat in the armchair there.

"Now, what can I do for you?" he asked.

"I don't want this to be generally known," Molly said, "but I represent an investor in Denver, and because you have been recommended to me as an important and knowledgeable man in Creede, I —"

"Now hold on," Drago said, eyeing her. "Are you telling me some fat cat in Denver sent a woman down here to —"

"Mr. Drago," Molly said with exaggerated

patience, "not all fat cats, as you call them, are men, as you seem to assume. My client happens to be a woman, and quite a wealthy one at that."

Drago paused. "Yeah? Who?"

"As I said, I don't want this to be generally known," Molly said, "but her name is Boatwright." She paused.

"Boatwright," Drago repeated. "Sure, I know that name. Boatwright. Mines in Leadville, right? Built a hell of a mansion on Capitol Hill."

Molly nodded. "Mrs. Boatwright's a widow now. Her husband died several years ago, as you may have heard."

"I never read the news of high society when I was in Denver," Drago said. "But the point is the old lady's looking for a way to make her money grow, right?"

"Yes," Molly said. "Her husband made a fortune with the right investments, and she hopes to do the same."

"I get the picture," he said. He eyed her. "You got a letter of credit?"

Molly smiled. "I believe you're getting ahead of matters, Mr. Drago. When I came here a week ago to look things over, I was impressed with the Orleans Club. After I returned to Denver, I suggested to Mrs. Boatwright that she invest in town properties rather than mining claims. They're less risky, I believe."

"You're dead right about that," Drago said. "Every miner and working man in the district has to spend money in Creede sooner or later. Plenty of men have gone broke and headed for home. They left their money behind, right here. And every passenger train brings in a fresh load."

"So I've noticed," Molly said. "That's why I'm looking around for the best investment properties, whether it's raw land or an established business. What I'd like to know from you is whether or not you have any properties for sale at the moment."

"Lady, everything I own is for sale," he said with a short burst of laughter. "You wanta buy the Orleans Club — it's yours. You wanta buy any of my other properties — they're yours. All we gotta do is talk price." He added, "After you show me a letter of credit."

Molly acknowledged this challenge with a nod. "Mrs. Boatwright deals in cash purchases. She will authorize me to invest a large sum in Creede when she is satisfied that I have found the right property. So, before we consider price, I must know precisely what properties are available."

"All right, I get the picture," he said. "No

sense in beating around the bush. How large a sum you talking about?"

Molly met his gaze. Lou Drago was a blunt man who possessed crude intelligence. She knew she would have to throw out some bait to capture his interest. "For her first investment, Mr. Drago, the sum will be in the neighborhood of one hundred thousand dollars."

Drago's eyes widened for a fraction of a second. He said casually, "Well, Mrs. Boatwright will find property values high down here, higher than in Denver." He paused deliberately. "I may have something that will be to her liking."

"I hope so," Molly said, sensing that he was hooked. "What are they?"

He shoved his chair back. "I'll show you, if you got time for a walk around town."

For the next hour Molly toured Creede at Drago's side. He showed her two saloons he owned, Miner's Luck and Second Chance, as well as two buildings on Creede Avenue, Webber's Sporting House and the Silver Splendor Theater. The latter was not a theater but a brothel with a stage and walkway where men selected their women from an hourly parade every afternoon and night. On Wall Street near the train depot Drago took Molly through a small hotel called the

Colorado House, where he owned a half-interest.

"Now, of course, you've seen my pride and joy, the Orleans Club," he said when they returned to the door of the San Juan Building. "I own that place free and clear."

"Haven't you sold stock in the Orleans Club?" Molly asked.

Drago gave her a long look. "You've been asking questions around here, haven't you?"

"It's my job," Molly said. "Mr. Drago, if we're going to do business, you'll have to tell me the straight, unvarnished truth. Have you sold stock certificates in the other properties you've shown me?"

"Right now that's none of your damned business," he said. "Listen, lady, when I tell you I own something free and clear, believe me, I do. I have the property deeds to prove it. Don't worry about any lies or rumors you've heard about stock certificates. When you show me cash, I'll show you property deeds. Understand?"

Molly nodded, surprised at this outburst. But by angering the man she had learned all that she wanted to know. Lou Drago had no intention of honoring the shares he had sold in the Orleans Club.

IX

For the next three days Molly used the teeming boardwalks of Creede as a cover while she observed the comings and goings in the saloons and brothels owned by Lou Drago. She stood in recessed doorways, paused in back alleys, or moved with the surging crowds up one street and down another, at times fending off leering men who had mistaken her for a streetwalker.

She got to know the camp very well and learned that within the chaos was a certain rhythm of life, a pulsation of humanity. It came with the end of day or night shifts at the mines and mills, when thirsty and hungry men flooded Creede Avenue. Another tidal wave swept through the camp every afternoon when the long D & RG passenger train rumbled to a halt at the depot and disgorged its human cargo.

Aside from the working men and the residents, Creede had more than its share of characters. Some were drunks who bummed tobacco and coins from passersby. Molly recognized one. He was the stout, shrill-voiced man who had caused the disturbance in the Olds Bros. Café. Seeing now that he made regular rounds of the saloons, she paused at enough open doors to find out that he caged drinks at the bars by telling stories that he was convinced were humorous and had the entertainment value of a shot or two. At each establishment, though, he soon wore out his welcome, and then he moved on to the next saloon.

One busy corner on Creede Avenue was often occupied by a scrawny man in a tattered black suit and stovepipe hat who called himself Preacher Ed. In a graveled, booming voice he beseeched the sinners to repent before it was too late. The end of the world was near, time was running out, and those who were not saved would burn in the fires of hell for all time. Despite ridicule and an occasional punch from a passing sinner, Preacher Ed called out his message morning, noon, and night.

Molly's surveillance, however, inadvertently proved that the flesh is weak, for in a back alley more than once she saw Ed leaning against the unpainted wall of a building, tipping a long-necked bottle to his mouth. He drank the "remedy" in long gulps.

"Medicine for the throat," Molly once overheard him call out to a drunk weaving down the alley. "The good Lord provides," Ed said between gulps, "yessir, He tends His Flock of believers . . . does indeed, yessir." And late one night she saw the unmistakable profile of Ed climbing the outside staircase of a brothel, no doubt carrying the Word to the needy.

Molly found that Drago's establishments were as busy as any in Creede, and evidently generated a great deal of cash. Lou Drago himself made daily trips from them to the Merchants & Miners Bank with armed guards at his side, carrying weighty leather grips in either hand.

Frequently on these trips to the bank Drago was accompanied by the city marshal, the tall, long-jawed man with a waxed mustache whom Molly had first seen in the aftermath of the knifing during her first visit to the Orleans Club. Something about the relationship between these two men, a hint of the employer giving orders to the loyal employee, made Molly recall Saul Philips's suggestion that Drago's method of working involved having well-placed men on his payroll.

The lawman was certainly well placed in this camp. Molly overheard enough conversations on the streets of Creede to know that he was feared, a man who had used his gun here several times. John Light was his name, and Molly heard that he had come to Creede from Texas less than a year ago. The timing coincided with Drago's arrival.

Molly telegraphed an inquiry to the Denver U.S. marshal's office, asking Saul Philips for any available information on a lawman named John Light.

During this time she kept an eye peeled for Dave Hughes, but did not see the gambler in any of the saloons or gaming parlors in the camp. She did not find out why until the second evening of her surveillance. Returning to the Fifth Avenue Hotel, she was startled by a figure lurking in the shadows beside the building.

"It's me. No need for that gun."

Molly's hand had instinctively darted to the handle of the .38 in the shoulder holster under her jacket. She withdrew her hand as he stepped up onto the boardwalk. "I wondered when you'd show up."

"Like a bad penny," he said with a grin.

"Where have you been?" Molly asked.

"In Upper Creede," Dave replied, "getting acquainted across a poker table with Roger Hall."

"Who's he?" Molly asked.

"An undistinguished young man," Dave said, "who's head-over-teacup in love with my daughter."

"I think you'd better tell me about this investigation of yours," Molly said.

"Now, there's no need to get testy with me," Dave said. "I just wanted to find out who this boy is. I'm not getting in your way."

Molly paused. "What have you found out?"

"He's like a million others," Dave replied. "Came here to make his fortune, spent all his money, and ended up working in a silver mine. Still thinks he's going to get rich, somehow."

"If he sits at your table," Molly said, "there isn't much chance of that, is there?"

Dave protested good-naturedly, "I don't have a table in this ramshackle camp. I'm just a working man who's between jobs."

"How long can you make that story stick?" Molly asked.

Dave shrugged. "A long time. There's plenty of gambling halls here, and a few thousand men who think they know a hell of a lot more about poker than they do. Dealers, too. Most of them are amateurs. That bunch in the Orleans Club couldn't spot a ringer if he wore a sign around his neck."

"You were in there?" Molly asked, anger rising in her.

Dave nodded. "Walked right past Sharon, and she didn't recognize me. Of course, I didn't stay long enough to let her get a close look."

"I don't think you need me, Dave," Molly said. "You're conducting your own investigation."

"Sure, I need you," he said, "now more than ever. Look, I know I was taking a chance by going into the Orleans Club, but I wanted to see the place for myself. And I wanted to see Sharon. You know, she doesn't look too healthy. I wonder if she's eating right."

Molly couldn't stay angry with him. His concern for his daughter was genuine. And he had charm. She said, "Sharon works long hours. Like most young people, she wants to make her fortune as soon as possible."

"I reckon so," Dave conceded. "Well, tell me, what have you found out about Lou Drago?"

Molly recounted the details of her meeting with the man, describing all the properties owned by Drago.

"I knew it," Dave said softly when she finished. "I had this thing figured right from the start. He sold phony shares in the Orleans Club and pocketed the money. One of these days he'll sell out and skip town."

"Could be," Molly said. "But he'll stay awhile. He's making a lot of money. Drago's a big man around this camp."

"So he'll ride this bronc as long as it bucks," Dave said. He added, "Or until someone runs him out of here."

"Are you that someone?" Molly asked.

Instead of answering, he grinned. Then he said, "I'm not going to do anything stupid, Molly. I won't do anything to endanger Sharon's life. But I will need you."

"To do what?" Molly asked.

"To go with me," he said, "when I meet Sharon face to face. I've decided to see her and try to talk some sense into her head."

"You don't need me for that," Molly said.

"Oh, yes, I do," Dave said. "I want you to tell her everything you've told me. Everything. She'll believe you —"

"She didn't the first time around," Molly said.

"But with the two of us," Dave said, "there's a chance we'll get through to her. Alone, I don't have much of a chance at all."

That was probably true. Molly thought this over while Dave looked at her intently. She decided it was worth one more try. "All right. How do you plan to go about this?"

"First thing in the morning," he replied, "I want you to take me to that shack she and Roger call home."

★ ★ ★

The next day Molly discovered that any
time between ten o'clock and noon was "first
thing in the morning" by Dave's standards.
She had risen early, eaten breakfast in the
hotel dining room, and gone into the lobby to
wait. Hours dragged past while she flipped
through and then read back issues of the illus-
trated magazine Cosmopolitan. By ten-thirty
she had learned about bee keeping, the tem-
perament of saleswomen in large clothing
stores, and read an Indian adventure story il-
lustrated by Frederic Remington.

Twenty minutes later the door swung open
and Dave Hughes strode in. "Been waiting
long?"

"A while," Molly allowed.

"Suppose you've had breakfast," he said,
looking toward the dining room.

"It's almost time for dinner, Dave," Molly
said.

"Oh," he said, turning his gaze back to her.
"You're an early riser, aren't you. Me, I generally don't get to bed until a couple hours
after midnight." He paused. "I wonder if
Sharon's up and around yet. Probably not.
Maybe we ought to hang around here for a
while. . . ."

Molly realized that he was very nervous.
The prospect of meeting Sharon face to face

must have been a frightening one to him, and now the slightest excuse would be enough reason for delay.

"Want to call the whole thing off?" Molly asked.

"No, no," he said irritably. He took a deep breath and then forced a smile. "Oh hell, might as well get it over with."

They left the hotel and made their way up the crowded boardwalk on Creede Avenue to Willow Creek Canyon. With a bright sun straight overhead in a clear blue sky, they followed the rutted freight road to the buildings of Upper Creede.

Molly led the way past the long, two-story boardinghouse along the footpath through the weeds to the log cabin. Dave followed her to the door, standing back a few paces as Molly rapped on it.

Sharon opened the door, and almost closed it when she saw Molly. But in the next moment Sharon's gaze went to the man behind her. She stared, and recognition seeped into her expression.

"Oh, no," she said softly. "Oh, no." For a long moment she seemed unable to take her eyes off her father, but then her expression hardened. Her gaze swung to Molly. "I told you not to bring him here."

Dave stepped forward. "Now, honey, don't

go blaming her. I could have found my way here on my own."

Sharon stared at him again, then her eyes swept over his worn and soiled clothes. "What are you up to?"

"We have to talk, Sharon," Dave said.

"No, we don't," she replied quickly.

"Hear me out," he said. "And listen to what Molly has to say. Then we'll leave — for good."

"I've heard what she has to say," Sharon said. "I know why you're here, and I know you're wrong about Lou. He's a good man, a smart man, and he's found a way for us all to make a lot of money."

"Dammit," Dave said, exasperated. "Those shares you bought in the Orleans Club are worthless. You'll never see a dime of that money you gave him. And you sure as hell don't know Lou Drago."

Sharon's face reddened at her father's anger, but she held her voice steady when she said, "Is that all you've got to say?"

"No!" He said forcefully. "I've got plenty more to say, and I want you to hear me out, young lady!"

Sharon shook her head.

"Now, you listen to me —" Dave began.

"No, I won't," she said. "I don't want to hear your lies — either of you. I want you

106

to leave me alone. Will you do that? Will you go back to Cheyenne and leave me alone?"

Molly saw Dave looking at his daughter with an incredulous expression on his clean-shaven face. He was clearly at a loss for words. He said nothing when Sharon backed into the doorway and closed the door.

Dave cursed angrily and rushed toward the plank door, hands outstretched as though he intended to pull it apart one board at a time.

"Dave," Molly said, "we'd better leave."

He shot an angry look at her as he reached the door.

"Give her time to think," Molly said. "And give yourself some time to cool off."

He slapped his hands together and swore again. Then he whirled around and strode away.

Molly followed him back to Creede, unable to walk fast enough to keep up. She saw Dave punch through the batwing doors of the Denver Exchange. When Molly reached the boardwalk there, she paused, then entered. She found the gambler at the bar, tilting a shotglass to his lips. The bartender had just set a bottle of rye whiskey in front of him, and now he watched as Molly moved in beside him.

"Let's go to a table," she said softly.

For a moment Dave Hughes did not acknowledge her presence, but then he nodded curtly and snatched up the long-necked bottle.

They went to a round table near the far wall and sat down. The Denver Exchange was similar to the Orleans Club in its arrangement. The front section was a saloon, and access to the gambling parlor in the rear was gained through a pair of double doors, now open.

"I went over it a million times in my mind," Dave said dully. "I knew what I was going to say. I knew just how it would go. But what happens? I lose my temper, and Sharon slams the door in my face."

Molly watched him refill the shotglass with amber whiskey. "It's agonizing to see someone you love making a terrible mistake."

"The damned, sad truth is that she acted like a grown woman while I was acting like a kid," he said.

"Maybe you should tell her that," Molly said.

He looked at her in surprise.

Molly went on. "Apologize and tell her that you love her, that you're proud of her."

A long moment passed while Dave considered the idea. Then he drained the shotglass. "She wants nothing to do with me, that's clear."

They sat in silence, with Dave Hughes staring at the label on the long-necked bottle, which read, OLD QUAKER CLUB MONONGAHELA RYE, ABSOLUTELY PURE. Then his attention was caught by raised voices and he looked up at the doorway to the gambling parlor.

Molly followed his gaze and saw a tall, dark-haired man there. He was politely but firmly inviting someone to leave.

"That's Masterson," Dave said.

"Who?" Molly asked, looking at the well-dressed man who wore a small mustache.

"Bat Masterson," Dave replied. "Runs this place for a Denver syndicate." A moment later Dave said, "Oh, no . . . not her."

Molly saw Bat Masterson grasp a feminine arm and pull a woman through the doorway. He forcefully escorted a big rangy woman through the saloon. In her rough voice she protested loudly all the way that she was not afraid of Bat Masterson or any other man in this stinking camp.

Dave had recognized her before Molly did, and now he slid down in his chair, groaning. The woman was Calamity Jane.

"At least she didn't see us," Dave said, staring at the flapping batwing doors through which Masterson had just shoved Calamity Jane out to the boardwalk. The gambler straightened up in his chair.

"What are you going to do next?" Molly asked.

Dave pulled his gaze from the doors and looked at her. "I was just thinking," he said in a subdued voice, "there isn't much I can do. Maybe I shouldn't have come down here in the first place. Maybe I was dreaming, seeing myself as a white knight coming to the rescue." He exhaled. "Sharon's got her mind made up. If she's decided she's old enough to make grownup decisions, then I reckon I ought to let her live with grownup consequences —"

After a long pause, Molly asked, "You're planning to leave Creede?"

Dave shrugged and shifted his absent gaze to the label on the bottle of rye whiskey. "Don't have anywhere to go. My table at the Stockmen's Inn has been taken over by another gambler." He looked at her again. "Well, it's over. I reckon you've done as much as you can. I appreciate the work you did for me. I know that from the beginning you figured this whole thing was harebrained."

"I thought your motives were right," Molly said.

A faint smile creased the corners of his eyes. "Well, that's something. I get the feeling you won't work for someone you don't like."

"Not if I can help it," Molly said. She reached out and lightly touched his arm. "Dave, I've come to realize that you're a good man."

"Thanks," he said. "I wish I could convince my daughter of that." He took a deep breath. "Maybe you're right. If I'd told her that I love her and that I'm proud of her, things might have turned out differently. And, by God, I am proud of her. She's down here in a tough camp, making her own way in a tough business. And from the way Roger Hall plays poker, she's probably buying his groceries, too. Now, how many seventeen-year-old girls could do that?"

"It's not too late to tell her that," Molly said, "but I suggest you leave out the part about her boyfriend."

Dave grinned, but then shook his head. "I think it is too late. Sharon's made up her mind about Lou Drago, and she's made up her mind about me."

"After she's had time to think," Molly said, "she may change her mind. Daughters always have special feelings for their fathers."

"I'm afraid I haven't given her much reason to have those feelings about me," Dave said. "But, hell, this is starting to sound like self-pity, isn't it? Must be getting drunk. Enough." He shoved the bottle away. "I reckon you'll be taking the morning train out of here."

Molly nodded, looking for a tinge of regret in his face. She saw only a glum expression.

"No reason for you to stay any longer," he said without conviction. "No reason at all." After a long moment he held out his hand.

Molly shook his hand. She felt his firm grip, and it lasted longer than a handshake that was strictly business.

"So long," he said.

"Good luck, Dave," Molly said.

Molly walked alone down Creede Avenue after leaving the Denver Exchange. She went to the depot and bought a ticket on the next day's passenger train, then returned to her room.

With her key the desk clerk at the Fifth Avenue Hotel handed her a telegraphed message that had just arrived. Molly quickly read it.

Miss Owens:

Description matches the J.L. who was charged with murder in Ft. Worth, Texas, last year. Beat the charge. Defended by a ranch syndicate after killing two squatters. In the past J.L. has worked as strike breaker for three mine companies in Rocky Mountains. If you can prove J.L. works for L.D., let me know at once.

Saul Philips, United States Marshal Denver, Colorado

Molly walked upstairs to her room. She stood at the window, telegraphed message in her hand, and looked outside as she thought about this case. She had been tantalizingly close to cracking it open, and now she had to walk away from it.

She had started to pack her suitcase when a knock came at the door. She opened it, half-expecting and wholeheartedly hoping to find Dave there. Instead, Lou Drago stood in the hall, hat shoved back on his head.

"Misrepresented yourself a bit, didn't you, Miss Owens," he said.

Molly tried to appear indignant when she said, "I beg your pardon, Mr. Drago?"

"I did some checking on you," he said, "and on widow Boatwright. Things ain't quite the way you said; no, not quite."

Molly's thoughts raced as she considered her options. She could tell Drago that as a Fenton operative she was expected in Denver and that if she did not arrive as scheduled . . .

"You handed me that high-toned speech about how I'd have to tell you the straight, unvarnished truth if we're gonna do business," he said, "and here all along you weren't being straight with me. Now, lady, I don't like that. Not one bit."

"Mr. Drago," Molly said, "I think you should leave."

"No, I ain't leaving," he said, bearded jaw jutting toward her. "See, I had a man in Denver look into matters. He talked to old lady Boatwright and found out she runs a boardinghouse in that mansion. And she said she has no idea of investing money in Creede — if she even has any to invest." He drew a breath. "So I'm onto you."

"Mr. Drago —" Molly began.

"I'm onto your game," he interrupted, "because old lady Boatwright gave you away. She let it slip that you have more money than she does — a whole lot more."

Molly felt her eyes widen, then she nearly laughed aloud. She could picture the scene: Mrs. Boatwright confronting some oily man at her door, telling him in no uncertain terms that she would never waste her money on some half-baked investment scheme in a mining camp.

"You should have told me from the start," Drago said, "that you're fixing to invest your own money."

Now Molly did smile. She could picture Mrs. Boatwright saying it: "Why, that Miss Molly Owens has more money to invest than I do. Now, get off my property!" Molly realized she had to play this out to the end.

"Mr. Drago," Molly said, "I've found that some men will try to take advantage of a woman in business dealings. So my practice is to let businessmen assume I am representing someone else. That way I can get a more objective view of a proposed transaction."

Drago shook his head. "You should have trusted me. No man likes to be lied to."

"Once I had made my decision," Molly said, "I was prepared to tell you that I represent myself."

"That a fact?" he said. He was angry, but in a strange twist he was now more convinced of her legitimacy than ever.

"Yes, it is," Molly said.

"That Boatwright mansion's full of rich women, from what I hear," Drago said. "You're probably good for the hunnerd thousand. But I'll tell you one thing, lady. Before we do business you'll have to show me a bank statement."

"Of course," Molly said.

"All right, then," he said with an air of finality, as though he had put her in her place and established his own superiority. He asked, "Is that why you're headed for Denver tomorrow?"

A chill ran up Molly's spine. "You seem to know quite a bit about me, Mr. Drago." When he didn't reply, she said, "You've been following me, haven't you?"

"Not exactly," Drago said. "My man saw you come out of Masterson's place, and he kept an eye on you until you got back here to the hotel. Then he told me where I could find you. That's all there is to it."

Molly wondered if that was all there was to it. Drago was suspicious enough of her to have had her story checked out in Denver. Now she wondered if she had been trailed all morning and been seen with Dave Hughes.

Drago asked, "Masterson tell you that place of his is for sale?"

Molly thought quickly and decided to use a bit of information she had learned from Dave. "You must know as well as I do, Mr. Drago, that Masterson only manages the Denver Exchange. I went in there to look the place over, just as I had the Orleans Club and your other properties. If I decide to make an offer, I'll tender it to the owners in Denver."

"Is that your plan?" he asked.

"To find out," Molly said evenly, "you'll have to put another hound on my trail."

Drago's expression darkened. "Listen to me, lady, and listen good. I have ways of finding out what I want to know, especially if I figure someone's trying to put one over on me. A few have tried, and they've paid the price."

"That sounds like a threat, Mr. Drago," Molly said, meeting his angry stare.

"Take it any way you like," he said. "But just don't forget it." He turned and strode down the hall, then his boots sounded on the stairs as he descended them.

Molly closed the door and took a deep breath. Drago's rage was as quick and as menacing as she had ever encountered in a man, and now she fully understood that his reputation for ruthlessness was well earned.

As she thought over the events of the last two days, she wondered if she would be leaving Dave Hughes out on a limb by catching the train tomorrow. If Drago linked her to the gambler, he might turn his anger toward Dave. She felt certain that she and Dave had not been followed when they had gone to Upper Creede, but they might have been seen together when they returned to town.

Yesterday Dave had implied that someone ought to run Drago out of Creede. While she didn't know what his plans were — and suspected that Dave himself didn't know what he would do next — she doubted that Dave would simply leave here, defeated. He had given up his table in the Stockmen's Inn to come here, and now too much was at stake for him to walk away. If Dave didn't have a plan at this moment, Molly felt certain he would soon devise one.

The idea of riding the morning train out of here was more troubling now than ever. The more she thought about this case, all its ramifications and all the lives she had become a part of, the more she realized she could not leave here with the nagging thought in the back of her mind that she might inadvertently have led Lou Drago straight to Dave. The gambler had to be warned.

She waited half an hour, then left the Fifth Avenue Hotel, walking briskly to the intersection at Creede Avenue. As she rounded the corner, a glance back over her shoulder confirmed her suspicion. Hackles rose in the back of her neck. A man in a dark blue suit and derby hat had been lounging outside the hotel doors. Now he was following her.

Molly continued up Creede Avenue, not immediately trying to elude Drago's man. She would do as she was no doubt expected to do — tour hotels, saloons, and gambling parlors as potential properties to purchase. This she did during the next two hours, including the Denver Exchange and the Orleans Club. Dave Hughes was not in any of them.

The man who followed was slightly built and had a patch of black mustache under his flat nose. He was not particularly good at his job. At times he stayed too close, was too obvious, and then fell back too far, briefly losing sight of her. More than once Molly slowed her pace on a crowded boardwalk while the man caught up, hurrying and craning his neck to catch sight of her again.

Molly started down a side street toward a

hole-in-the-wall saloon when gunshots erupted inside the place. Men spilled out. The crowd outside momentarily froze, then turned toward the saloon, straining to see where the shots had come from.

As Molly halted, she witnessed the same phenomenon she had seen during the fight in the Orleans Club when she had first confronted Sharon Hughes. The curious onlookers who were trying to see what had happened collided with those who were just as eagerly seeking safety. More shots were fired, and confusion became pandemonium.

Taking advantage of the confusion, Molly ducked back through the crowd, circling around until she stood across the street and far behind the man who had followed her. His attention was fixed on the door of the saloon.

Molly looked over there and saw a big man in railroader's overalls writhing on the boardwalk, one hand grasping his thigh. Bright red blood seeped through his fingers. Clenched in his other hand was a small, dark revolver, and now shrieks and shouts came from the crowd as the railroader raised himself and aimed toward the open doorway of the saloon.

With the other onlookers Molly stared in horror at the railroader. He fired, cocked the gun and fired again, and then squeezed off a third shot. Stumbling through the doorway came a teamster, bare-headed, walking loose-legged as though drunk. But he was not drunk. At his bulging stomach blood seeped through his flannel shirt. He stood over the railroader, swaying slightly.

The teamster held a revolver. He deliberately aimed it down at the prone man. The gun bucked as it roared, and the railroader was thrown back with the impact. He lay still. The teamster's knees buckled and he sank to the boardwalk, falling face down beside the railroader.

A great stillness followed, broken only by Marshal John Light. The lawman pushed and elbowed his way through the crowd. He strode to the two bleeding men, his gun hand hovering near the walnut grips of his Peacemaker. He circled the downed men warily, and kicked their guns away from their limp hands.

"What happened here?" He shouted into the doorway of the saloon.

An aproned bartender appeared there. His shaky voice carried across the silent crowd to Molly's ears. "They . . . they was gambling and got to fighting over this woman. . . ."

"What woman?" Light demanded.

"She was playing cards with 'em," he said,

looking around. "Dunno where she ran off to . . . oughta be around here somewhere. . . ."

Molly was aware of movement behind her, but before she could turn around the sharp point of a knife jabbed into her side. A rough whisper, unmistakably feminine, came into her ear.

"Walk away with me," she hissed, "and make like we're together so that lawdog don't try to pin this thing on me."

Molly recognized the voice. She turned her head far enough to see the big woman at her side, and remembered a remark made by Dave Hughes: *Where there's trouble, there's Calamity.*

XI

Arm in arm with Calamity Jane, Molly was ushered away from the scene of the shootings. They made their way through the people swarming out of Creede Avenue to this side street, crowds of the curious drawn here by the explosive sounds of gunfire. Back at the saloon Molly heard the commanding voice of Marshal John Light as he sought witnesses. She looked back there, seeing Drago's man in the crowd, too, his back to her, mesmerized by tragedy like all the others.

When they reached Creede Avenue, Calamity Jane took Molly down the boardwalk to the next intersection and hauled her around the corner. Halting, she shoved Molly against the plank side of a hardware store, still holding the knife against her.

Breathing hard, Calamity Jane said, "I didn't know how in hell I was going to get out of there until I spotted you. Never was so surprised to see a familiar face in a crowd." She drew a deep, rasping breath as she quickly looked around. "I knew if I ran out of there, I'd never make it."

Molly had been surprised, too. She was so intent on dodging Drago's man that she had not seen Calamity Jane slip out of the saloon and plunge into the gathering crowd.

"If you're down here," Calamity Jane went on, "that means Dave is, too. Where is he?"

"Miss Canary —" Molly began.

"So you recollect my right name, do you?" she said. "Well, that's good, fancy lady, so long as you don't give me any of them yellow-bird jokes. I've heard them all, and don't like a one of them. Now, where's Dave?"

"Miss Canary," Molly said, feeling the knife press against her, "you seem to have the wrong idea about Dave Hughes and me —"

"The hell you say," Calamity Jane said. She brought the knife up and moved it close to Molly's throat. "You ain't the first and you won't be the last woman who's follered that man from one boom camp to another. He'll use you, but he'll never give his heart to you. I know that for a fact, and I know for a fact that you won't believe a word I'm saying. They never do. So go ahead, chase after him. Let him take his pleasure with you. But you can be sure of one damn thing — he's mine! Now, where is he?"

Molly looked into the woman's wild eyes. "You'll stab me if I don't tell you?"

The bulging eyes blinked. Calamity Jane

looked at the gleaming knife blade as though just then remembering it was there. She lowered it. "Why, hell no. I don't want you bleeding all over the place, soiling my dress and such." She thrust the knife into her beaded handbag. "Look, just save yourself some pain and tell me where he is."

"I don't know where Dave is," Molly said. "That's the truth."

"Truth," she said, disgusted. "The way women will lie for that man. I'll never understand why they do it."

"I'm not lying," Molly said.

"Even after he's used them and left them behind," Calamity Jane said, "women'll still lie for the no-good bastard." She glowered at Molly. "No, I don't need a frog-sticker to get the truth out of you. All I need is my bare hands." She raised one to Molly's face, fingers arching into claws.

"I wouldn't advise that," Molly said.

Calamity Jane grinned, showing teeth yellowed from plug tobacco. "No sense in getting yourself bruised up, fancy lady. Tell me what I want to know, and I'll walk away."

"If you try to harm me," Molly said, "you won't be able to walk away."

"Now, that's tough talk coming from little Miss Innocence," she said. She straightened her right hand, drew it back, and slapped

Molly across the face.

Molly saw the blow coming but did not try to block it. Her cheek stung, and tears came to one eye. "You just made a mistake."

"No, you're the one who's making a mistake," Calamity Jane said, "by not telling me what I want to know. Now, am I gonna have to hurt you to find out —"

Seeing the woman draw her hand back for another slap, Molly quickly ducked, cocking her fist back as she did so. From a half-crouched position she threw a short, powerful punch to the woman's ample midsection, burying her fist deep into the solar plexus.

A deep cry of anguish came from Calamity Jane's mouth. Molly stepped back. The big woman doubled over, her mouth and eyes stretched open as she slowly fell to the weathered planks of the boardwalk. She lay there, gasping.

Molly knelt beside her. "I warned you not to harm me," she said. "Now that I have your attention, listen to me. Don't ever pull a knife on me again. Don't ever threaten me. From this day on, stay out of my way. Hear me?"

Calamity Jane closed her mouth. Staring at Molly, she swallowed hard and nodded.

Molly straightened up and looked around. The altercation here had gone unnoticed as passersby were intent on seeing what had created the commotion in the next block. Molly waited several moments until Calamity Jane had managed to stand, hands pressed to her middle. She leaned against the wall of the hardware store, head bowed. Then Molly walked away, heading for the Fifth Avenue Hotel.

After supper in the hotel dining room, Molly waited until nightfall, then left through a back entrance. By the faint light of stars and a white sliver of moon she followed the alley to the point where it joined Creede Avenue at the mouth of Willow Creek Canyon. There she walked along the freight road through the dark canyon to Upper Creede.

Passing Sharon's cabin, Molly noted that the one window cut into the front of the log structure was dark. Sharon was undoubtedly working her shift in the Orleans Club at this hour. The man she lived with, Roger Hall, was either asleep in there or was leaning against a bar somewhere. At this early hour Molly guessed that the young man was out with his friends in a saloon or gambling hall.

Ahead Molly saw a splash of lamplight on the rutted road. From a false front hung a sign picturing a mug of beer with a foaming head. Molly walked toward the saloon, angling across the road to the door. Through a window she saw men inside, miners from their appearance, in light clouded with cigar and pipe smoke. She opened the door and went in.

Straight in front of her was a plank bar supported by whiskey barrels at either end. No tables or chairs were in the place, and as Molly ventured in she realized she was the only woman in this watering hole. Husky men with rounded shoulders wore flannel shirts and cotton duck or denim trousers, and some still wore rubber boots from work. They all had stopped in mid-sentence or mid-drink to turn and look at her.

"Hunting a runaway husband, betcha," one of the miners at the bar said. The room had fallen quiet, and he turned away as he realized he had spoken louder than he had intended.

"No," Molly said, smiling as she stepped toward the middle of the smoke-filled room. "I'm looking for a man who might have been playing cards in here. He wears khaki work clothes with green suspenders, and he's clean-shaven with short hair, sandy in color. Any of you gentlemen seen him?"

"Maybe," a bearded miner said around a cheek bulging with tobacco. "What's the feller's name?"

"I don't know what name he's traveling under," Molly said. "Has he been here tonight?" When no one replied, she added, "He's not my husband, and I don't plan on shooting him."

The men chuckled over the remark, but then fell silent again. They stared at her, regarding her as a woman.

At last the bartender said, "No, I reckon not. There isn't much gambling in here, ma'am."

"Well, thank you, gentlemen," Molly said.

"By God, I wish you was looking for me," one of the men ventured.

Molly answered with a smile on her way out. As she stepped outside, she took a deep breath of the cool, fresh night air. She felt reasonably certain that Dave had not been in that place tonight, if ever.

Farther up the road she saw another band of yellow light and realized that it might be coming from the windows of another saloon or gambling hall. She started in that direction, but had gone only half a dozen paces when the saloon door behind her opened and a man spoke to her. Turning, she saw a bearded man come out. He closed the door and moved toward her.

"You're Miss Owens, aren't you?"

Molly reached under her jacket and

wrapped her fingers around the grips of her revolver. The man stopped six or seven feet away. Lamplight shone on his face, illuminating his trimmed beard and the angle of his nose, and casting a gleam in his gray eyes.

"Do I know you?" Molly asked, ready to draw her revolver. The thought had crossed her mind that this could be one of Drago's men.

"No, ma'am, you don't," he replied, "but I've heard plenty about you. You fit Sharon's description to a T."

Molly moved her hand away from the gun. "You must be Roger Hall."

"That's right," he said.

"I doubt that you've heard anything good about me," Molly said.

He smiled. "I'll put it this way. Sharon admires you. She told me you're a woman who gets things done. And you live well, too, the way she wants to."

Molly was surprised to hear that assessment from Sharon Hughes, and she was also surprised at this first impression of Roger Hall. He seemed intelligent and he had a reserved, polite way about him.

"The gambler you said you're looking for," Roger went on, "is Sharon's father, I take it."

"That's right," Molly said. "Have you seen him?"

"Not this evening," he replied. "But I have played poker with him, so I know what he looks like." He paused. "Across that card table I didn't know who he was. I suppose he wanted it that way. I don't imagine he approves of my living arrangement with Sharon."

"To tell you the truth, Roger," Molly said, "I don't know of any father who would."

"I understand that," he said. "But Sharon and I love one another, and she's safe with me. Not many single women around here feel safe — unless they can afford to live in the Fifth Avenue Hotel."

"You've got a point there," Molly conceded.

"I'm fairly certain Dave Hughes isn't here in Upper Creede tonight," he said. "There are only two other saloons here, and I stopped off at both of them before I came down to this one about an hour ago." He added, "More money is changing hands down in Creede."

"But none of yours," Molly said.

Roger smiled, his teeth gleaming white in the lamplight. "I learned my lesson the hard way. Guess it's a common story around here."

"I'd like to hear it," Molly said.

Roger gazed at her a moment, then said, "My partner and I came to Creede with our life savings in our pockets and big ideas about going into the mining business. We'd both taken classes at Colorado School of Mines and had some ideas about where to look for outcroppings of silver. But we hardly got past Creede Avenue. I lost my stake gambling and my pard lost his to a perfumed woman who left him in a back alley with a knot on his head. He caught a freight out of here the next night. I stayed on, but now I work for somebody else at three and a half dollars a day, live in a grubby little cabin, and every Sunday — no matter how tired I am — I go out prospecting." He paused. "The only good part of the story is Sharon. Weren't for her, I'd have pulled out long ago."

Molly liked Roger Hall. He had an openness about him and spoke with candor.

"Mind if I ask why you're hunting for Dave Hughes?" he asked.

Molly regretted that she couldn't be as candid as he'd been. "I have a message for him — an important one."

"I see," he said, and waited for her to elaborate. When she did not, he said, "If I see him, I'll tell him to get ahold of you."

"Thanks," Molly said. "Nice meeting you, Roger."

After they parted, Molly checked the other establishments in Upper Creede and found that he had been right. Dave was not here, and no one had seen him tonight. She walked back down the canyon to Creede, back to the din of brass bands and pianos, saloon barkers, and the beckoning calls of prostitutes. *Dave must be here somewhere,* she thought.

But as the night wore on she was unable to locate him or any trace of him. By midnight she had walked through nearly every saloon and dance hall and gaming parlor at least once, including the Orleans Club, where Sharon was hard at work behind a twenty-one table, and Molly had given a description of Dave to more than a dozen hotel desk clerks and an equal number of owners of rooming houses on the fringe of town. None had seen the man.

Molly returned to her room in the Fifth Avenue Hotel, footsore and exhausted. She took off her high button shoes and slumped down on the bed, trying to think how she could have missed Dave tonight. She felt certain that he was still in Creede. Perhaps she had overlooked him in some gambling den, or maybe he was in a rooming house she had missed. . . .

But that was unlikely. She knew Dave Hughes well enough to know that he would be practicing his livelihood somewhere tonight, and he should have been seated at a round, felt-covered table in one of the gambling parlors she had passed through.

But then a chill ran up her spine as another explanation for his disappearance came to mind. Perhaps the gambler had been lured into a trap — one that had been set by Lou Drago.

XII

Molly slept fitfully through the night and awoke early. After breakfast in the hotel dining room, she walked hurriedly up Willow Creek Canyon to Sharon's cabin.

A sleepy-eyed Sharon Hughes opened the door and looked dully at Molly, as she might regard an unwelcome guest. Before she could speak, Molly said, "I'm looking for your father."

"So I hear," Sharon said. "Roger told me this morning."

"Have you seen your father in the last twenty-four hours?" Molly asked.

"You don't learn very fast, do you," Sharon said irritably. "If you'd been paying attention, you'd know by now that I don't care if I never see him again."

Molly replied with rising anger, "And what if you don't?"

"Just what do you mean by that?" Sharon asked.

"I mean you've been playing the high and mighty role," Molly replied, "and I think it's about time you climbed off that pedestal."

"What the hell are you talking about?" Sharon demanded. She turned her hands palms up. "I don't know why I'm even listening to you."

"I happen to know that you came to Creede with a pocketful of your father's money," Molly said. "And you act like he's spent his life trying to hurt you. You may have been hurt as a child, but your father thought he was doing his best by you. You're old enough to realize that and leave the past behind. You want to be treated like an adult? Act like one."

"Get out!" Sharon shouted. She took a step back and flung the door shut.

Molly stood there for several moments, her face hot. She had not lost her temper, as Dave had made the mistake of doing, but delivering a lecture had not been the right approach either. Somehow she should have befriended Sharon. She needed the young woman's help, or at least her cooperation. Molly would get neither now.

The distant blast of a steam engine's whistle reminded Molly that the daily passenger train would soon be departing. She walked away from the cabin and started down the freight road toward Creede. The whistle sounded again, seeming more insistent this time.

No, I've made up my mind, Molly thought.

I'm not leaving until I find Dave — or find out what happened to him.

Molly renewed her search, and throughout the morning she gave a description of Dave to bartenders and to the proprietors of rooming houses and hotels. She also interviewed several gamblers in Creede's gaming houses. By noon she was again footsore and tired, and had uncovered no solid leads. Dave Hughes had not been seen in this town in the last twenty-four hours. Molly was convinced of that now.

But there was one new development. Late in the morning Molly noticed that she was again being followed by the man in the dark blue suit and derby hat. He watched from a distance as she moved from one Creede Avenue establishment to another.

Molly had just about decided what to do about him when a pair of funeral hearses came rumbling down the main street. Drawn by sleek black horses, the glass-sided vehicles each bore a casket. They were driven by men dressed in black who stared straight ahead. Molly watched the hearses roll past and head for the cemetery on a sloping hillside outside of town. In the caskets, no doubt, were the two men who had settled their dispute with guns yesterday.

For some reason, the sight of those black

hearses stirred Molly to action. As she turned away and headed for the back alley behind Creede Avenue, she realized the thought had crossed her mind that if Dave Hughes was carried away in one of those gleaming black vehicles she would blame herself.

In the alley that bordered Willow Creek, Molly ducked into a narrow passageway between two frame buildings. She drew her revolver and waited.

Presently she heard the crunch of footfalls, and knew by the sounds that he was coming her way. The moment he appeared, she thrust the gun toward the side of his head.

"Stop right there," she said.

Startled, the man jumped and whirled toward her. Molly came out of the passageway, and he backed away.

"I told you to stop, mister," Molly said, "and I mean it. Don't make me use this gun."

The man's mouth curved into a scowl, twisting his small mustache. "You wouldn't shoot me."

"I won't," Molly said, "if you answer some questions."

He stood still for a long moment, then shook his head curtly. "I got nothing to say to you, and I'm betting you won't shoot a man in the back." With that he turned and started to walk away.

Her bluff called, Molly thrust the revolver back into her shoulder holster. She lunged after the man, her pent-up anger rising like steam in a boiler.

The man heard her coming and half-turned just as Molly reached him. She grasped his shoulder, but too late saw his fist coming around his body. The blow struck her above the ear, and Molly went down.

She rolled in the dirt and came up on her knees. She felt light-headed. Looking up at the man, she saw a strange smile on his face, as though he had never slugged a woman before, but had enjoyed it.

"Want me to hit you some more, lady?" he asked. "That what you want? You like being roughed up?"

Molly gave her head a shake, not so much to answer the questions but to clear her head. The man had punched her very hard, and she had walked right into it. Now she struggled to her feet.

Standing before him, Molly tried to speak, but was too dazed to focus her thoughts. She swayed, and almost fell again.

"Sleepy, ain't you?" he said, laughing. He reached out and grasped her arm, plunging his other hand under her jacket. "Reckon I'd better relieve you of that shiny gun you were waving at me."

Molly felt his hand roughly brush over her breasts, then saw him pull her revolver out of her shoulder holster. Reacting by instinct, she grabbed that wrist with both hands.

"So what d'you think you're doing now?" he asked, laughing again.

Molly took a deep breath. Her head was clearing, and in that instant she knew she would be able to translate thought into action.

She thrust his arm upward, stepped under it, and brought it down swiftly. The man was lifted off his feet as he spun around in midair, landing flat on his back. With a grunt, the air rushed out of him.

The revolver had fallen from his grasp and now lay in the dirt a few feet away. Molly went for it, but the man had recovered enough to get his boot under her feet and trip her. Molly went to her knees, falling forward on both hands.

"Damn you," he growled.

Molly rose as he scrambled toward her, his nostrils flaring and his mouth twisted with rage. She did not have time to stand or escape, so she met him head on. In that fraction of a second she thought they must look like a pair of warring animals, down on all fours in the dirt, growling and breathing hard in mortal combat.

They came together in a rising cloud of dust, and Molly felt the superior strength of the man as he reached out and grasped her forearm, yanking her toward him. Using a principle of jujitsu, Molly yielded until he drew back as far as he could, and then she shoved, using her weight to push him back.

The maneuver worked perfectly, and the man, bigger and stronger, was thrown back. He quickly straightened up, but was an instant too late to avoid Molly's elbow, which she had thrust toward his neck. The point of her elbow caught him squarely on the Adam's apple, and he dropped like a sack of grain, gasping.

Molly got to her feet, retrieved her revolver, and came back to the prone man. His dark suit was covered with dust, and his derby hat, dented and dirty, lay beside him. Molly quickly searched him for a weapon and found a pocket derringer in his trousers. She unloaded it, tossed the small bullet into Willow Creek, and dropped the gun beside his hat.

"Who sent you?" Molly asked.

The man answered with a cough as he looked up at her. His breath came in rasps.

Molly jammed the pointed toe of her shoe into his ribs. "Answer my question, mister, unless you want more of the same."

At last he sat up, gingerly touching his throat with his fingertips. He coughed again and then said one word: "Drago."

"Why does Lou Drago want me followed?" Molly asked.

The man looked up at her, grimacing as he swallowed. "He never told me."

"You work for him?" Molly asked.

The man nodded.

"Doing what?" she asked.

"Whatever needs doing," he said.

"He wouldn't give you a job to do without telling you something about why he wants it done," Molly said.

"Sure he would," he replied. "He does all the time." He coughed again. "For all I know, you owe Lou money."

Molly was inclined to believe him. This man was in pain and had seen enough trouble for one day. She knelt beside him.

"I have a question to ask you, mister," she said, "and if you give me a straight answer, our business will be finished. We'll go our separate ways. Understand?"

He nodded as he regarded her.

"Have you roughed up any men lately?" Molly asked.

"No," he said. He added, "I don't do that kind of stuff."

"But Drago has men who does," Molly said. "I'm asking if you know about any jobs like that."

"No, not lately," he said.

"Maybe you know indirectly of a man who's been killed," Molly suggested. "A clean-shaven man in work clothes with green suspenders, a man who keeps his hair cropped short."

"No," he said, shaking his head. "I don't know anything about a killing." He looked at her intently. "That's the God's truth, lady."

"It had better be," Molly said. They stared at each other for several moments, then Molly straightened up. She turned and walked away, brushing dirt and dust from her dress. Her hair had come unpinned, and as she walked out of the alley she realized she must look terrible, as though she had just come away from a fight.

XIII

After a bath and change of clothes in the Fifth Avenue Hotel, Molly ate a quick meal and resumed her search. This time she stayed on the boardwalks of Creede Avenue and the busiest side streets, thinking that if she had somehow missed Dave before, she would certainly see the gambler among the thousands of men coming and going in the heart of town.

But by sundown she felt as though she had seen every man in Creede except Dave Hughes. While standing in the recessed doorway of a dress shop she had seen Lou Drago making his rounds with a pair of burly, dour-faced men at his side. She saw other familiar faces pass by, among them Bat Masterson, Marshal John Light, and Calamity Jane. None of these people noticed her, which was the way she wanted it.

But her presence had not gone unnoticed. She passed a Chinese laundry and hunched her shoulders against a cold breeze that swept out of Willow Creek Canyon. She turned down a side street and approached

144

the door of the Second Chance, a saloon and gambling parlor.

Just as Molly remembered that the Second Chance was one of the saloons owned by Drago, she saw that the front door was closed and the windows were curtained. Earlier in the afternoon this saloon had been open. But before she could make sense of this she heard heavy footfalls and an instant later was grabbed from behind by a pair of strong arms. The saloon door swung open and she was thrust inside, the door slamming shut behind her.

The abduction had taken a few seconds, no more, and Molly doubted that anyone on the side street was aware of what had happened. She stood in the dark room while rough hands slid over her body and took away her revolver and handbag.

"Okay, Lou," the man said.

In the darkness at the back of the room a match flared, and Molly saw Lou Drago bring the flame in his fingertips to the wick of a lamp. The kerosene lamp stood on the back bar in front of a large mirror, along with rows of bottles stacked glasses, and mugs, and as Molly looked back there she saw Drago in double image. He replaced the lamp's glass chimney and turned to face her, his hat pushed high on his forehead.

"Thought you were leaving town, Miss Owens," he said.

Molly moved toward him half-a-dozen paces, looking around. "Did you empty this place out on my account, Mr. Drago?"

"I'll ask the questions," he said. He leaned against the bar, studying her. "I thought this was as good a place as any for us to have a little talk, so I cleared the room out, figuring you'd come by, sooner or later. You've been walking the boardwalks of this town since you roughed up Sammy, haven't you?"

"I defended myself from a man who persisted in following me, Mr. Drago," Molly said.

"Persisted in following you," he repeated. "Damned if you don't talk good." He came around the bar. "Now it's time for you to drop the act you're putting on so we can get down to cases. I've got two simple questions for you, and I want answers to them — right now. Who are you, and what the hell are you doing here in Creede?"

"Mr. Drago, I've told you my name and I've told you the nature of my business in Creede —"

Molly saw him nod once to the man behind her, but the only warning she had was the quick whisper of a boot heel on the bare

146

floor. In the next instant she was down, her head ringing.

"Pick her up," Drago said.

Molly felt the man's hands slide under her arms, and then she was lifted from the floor to a standing position. Her knees were rubbery and her ears rang. She just now understood that she had been slugged from behind, either with a fist or a sap.

"Miss Owens," Drago said, standing close to her now, "I know a couple things about you. I know you carry a .38. I know you somehow whipped a grown man. Now, that don't add up to make you a woman who's looking for investment properties, and I don't wanta hear that lie anymore. If I do, Henry back there is gonna bang you again, only harder. This ain't a game with me, it's business. Now talk, and talk right."

"I think you know why I'm here," Molly said.

"Maybe I do," he said, "but I want to hear it from you. Answer my question: Who are you and what are you?"

Molly was aware of the man behind her, waiting for the next signal from Drago. She drew a deep breath and said, "I'm an operative for the Fenton Investigative Agency."

Drago's eyes widened. "A detective, a damned detective. And a lady one, at that. I'll be damned. Who sent you down here? Who's out to get me? Somebody from Denver?"

Molly shook her head.

"Who?" he demanded. "Who is the scum?"

"I don't know," Molly said.

Drago scowled, and started to signal the man behind her.

"No need to hit me again," Molly said. "I'm telling you the truth. I've never been told who's paying for the reports I send back to New York." She watched his face as she spoke, seeing a look of deep suspicion there. The lie was the best she could come up with on short notice, and in a weird way there was an element of truth in it. At the moment she was not working for anyone.

"I don't believe you," Drago said.

"It's the only answer I've got," Molly said. "I'm not going to invent a name just to keep your man from hitting me again." Molly saw his expression change slightly, and knew she had convinced him.

"All right, then," he said. "What kind of reports are you sending back East on me?"

"Just about the properties you own in Creede," she said, "and how many people work for you."

"Who the hell wants to know that?" he demanded, then swore in exasperation. "Damn! This makes me mad. Some bastard's spying on me. Well, I tell you one thing. Whoever's doing this is out of business. You're on the next train out of here, lady." He jerked his head toward the man behind Molly. "Take her into the back room."

Grabbed from behind again, Molly was shoved through the saloon to an open door behind the bar. She was aware that Drago had picked up the lamp and followed, because light from it cast their distorted shadows on the floor and wall in front of them.

She was taken to a storeroom filled with beer barrels and wooden boxes containing whiskey and wine bottles. Pushed inside, she nearly fell as she careened off a barrel, But she caught her balance and turned to face the doorway. Drago stood there, smirking, lamp in hand.

"You're getting off lucky, detective lady," he said, "so's I can prove a point. Nobody can investigate me and get away with it. Put that in your final report, hear?" He paused. "In the morning when I take you to the train, think about how lucky you are to be alive."

Drago stepped back and closed the door. In the darkness Molly heard the sounds of a padlock thrust through a hasp, followed by a metallic *click*. A moment later the sounds of boots on the bare floor faded away.

The darkness was almost complete, and so was the silence. For a makeshift prison, this appeared to be a good one. The absence of street sounds made her realize that no amount of screaming would draw attention here. Evidently Drago intended to keep the Second Chance closed for the rest of the day and all night, and then early in the morning he expected to escort a frightened woman to the depot where the passenger train waited.

As Molly's eyes adjusted, a sliver of light caught her attention. She looked up and saw that it came from the ceiling straight overhead. She went to the door and felt for the handle. Finding it, she turned it and shoved. The door did not budge, as she expected. Then she ran her fingers all the way around the edge of the door, as a blind person would explore strange surroundings. She found no weakness that could be exploited.

Molly stepped back and considered her options. Drago had taken her revolver and her handbag. But he had not searched her. While she did not have skeleton keys and lock probes, she did have the two-shot derringer strapped to her thigh. She had considered using it before Drago closed the door, but the moment had not been right. She could ill afford a shootout with two armed men with such a small weapon. In the morning, though, she might catch Drago alone.

But she didn't want to wait that long if she could avoid it. She desperately wanted to continue her search for Dave Hughes, and the sooner she could break out of here, the better.

Molly made a complete search of the storeroom, feeling her way around the beer barrels and stacked boxes. The results were discouraging. The room had no windows, and the only exit was the locked door.

She did come across a mallet, the kind bartenders used to pound bungs into beer barrels. Holding this wooden mallet in her hand, she looked up at the sliver of light overhead. She realized that it came through a gap in the boards of a false ceiling, ten or twelve feet up. Wondering what was up there, she thought of a way to find out.

Molly went to the front of the storeroom and took a box of wine bottles off a stack. She placed it on the floor in the middle of the room, and got another. She put the two boxes side by side, and then a third one on top. In this way she built stairsteps toward the ceiling with ten boxes, four high at the top.

Molly climbed her staircase and stood on the top box. She reached up. Her hands touched the ceiling. She pushed. The board creaked, and the sliver of light widened for a brief moment. Molly climbed down and brought more boxes, making her staircase higher. Then she stepped up to the top again, this time with the mallet in hand.

She reached overhead and pounded the board until it came loose. Then she hit the boards, on either side of it. When the nails came out, she pushed the boards away. Straight up she saw the rafters of the building's roof.

Molly climbed down. She carried more boxes and fashioned a higher staircase that led up to the hole in the ceiling. Then she climbed out of the storeroom and crawled across the flat ceiling to the edge.

This storeroom was a large box that had been constructed in the rear of the building. Its sole purpose was to provide locked storage space. Daylight came from the front of the saloon.

Molly swung over the edge and let herself down the side, dropping to the floor. She walked around the outside wall of the storeroom to the doorway that led into the saloon. A gap in the curtained window by the front door was the source of the light she had seen.

A dark shape on top of the bar caught her eye, and Molly recognized her handbag. She went to it and picked it up, finding her revolver underneath it. She spun the cylinder while holding the gun to the light, and saw that it was still loaded.

Molly went to the front window. She looked out through the gap in the curtains, seeing men pass by on the boardwalk. Long shadows stretched across the side street. She judged that an hour or more had passed since she had been abducted.

Molly backed away from the window, thinking about what she should do. Her eyes went to the saloon door, and the lock under the handle. She could pick that lock and leave through the front door. But then she would run the risk of running up against Drago or one of his men on the street.

She turned and walked through the saloon, passing through the doorway behind the bar. She turned at the back storeroom and made her way through the darkness to the rear of the building. As she suspected, she found a rear entrance there, a heavy, oversized sliding door where beer barrels destined for the storeroom were rolled into the building. Molly fumbled in the darkness, and her probing hands found a padlock above the door handle.

She reached into her handbag and brought out a set of lock probes. Made of high-quality spring steel, the probes resembled dentist tools that curved to a small, flat surface at the end. Molly had been trained to use them by an expert locksmith in New York. Now she worked in the dark, finding the probe that slipped smoothly into the keyhole.

Bringing upward pressure to bear, she slowly drew the probe out of the lock. With a soft *click,* the mechanism released and the padlock sprung open. Molly lifted the lock off the iron ring anchored to the door and pulled the hasp away. Then she grasped the door handle and shoved. The door slid open several inches, creaking on its rollers.

Molly eased out, seeing that the alley behind the Second Chance was empty. She followed the narrow alley in the opposite direction from Creede Avenue, coming out on the next street, where the railroad tracks ran. She followed the rails toward the mouth of Willow Creek Canyon.

Molly walked hurriedly, glancing back to see that no one followed. She could not afford to meet up with Drago or any of his men. A place to hide until nightfall was what she needed. She knew of only one that was close and yet would take her away from town. Now hearing the gurgling sounds of the creek that flowed out of the mountains, Molly moved quickly into the cool shadow of Willow Creek Canyon.

XIV

Molly's knock on the door of the low cabin was answered by Roger Hall. Still wearing his muddy boots and mud-spattered work clothes, he looked at Molly in surprise, then invited her in.

"I just came off shift," he said, closing the door behind her, "and Sharon left for work an hour ago."

"I didn't come here to see her," Molly said, glancing around the interior of the sparsely furnished cabin. She turned and faced the young man. "I need a place to lay low until dark, and this seemed like a good one."

"Sounds like you've got trouble," Roger said.

"Some," Molly allowed. She added, "But I don't think Sharon would welcome me. I can move on. I certainly have no intention of dragging you into this."

"If it involves Sharon or her father," he said, "then I'm in it, too. Tell me what's going on. Did you ever locate Dave?"

"No," Molly said. "That's the beginning

155

of a long story. Sure you want to hear it?"

"I am," Roger replied. He cast a glance toward the black cast-iron stove on the far wall. "But first, let's do something about supper. Been a long time since I emptied my lunch bucket, and I'm getting a bit thin." He added, "And I'll bet you haven't eaten yet, either."

"I've been too busy," Molly said with half a smile.

"Then let's go to it," he said, heading for the stove. "I was just stoking up a fire when you knocked. I can't offer anything fancy, just venison and a batch of fried potatoes and greens."

"Sounds good," Molly said. "What can I do to help?"

"Nothing," he said. "Just take a seat at the table, and tell me that long story."

Fried venison steaks and sliced potatoes, gleaming with melting butter, were on the table by the time Molly finished telling Roger what had happened to her since she had first met him less than twenty-four hours ago. They ate in silence, then Roger pushed his chair back, cradling a cup of steaming coffee in both hands.

"Sharon won't believe this," he said at last. "Not a word of it."

"Do you?" Molly asked.

Roger nodded. "I haven't tied my star to Drago's wagon like she has. I won't even work for the man."

"He offered you a job in one of his saloons?" Molly asked.

Roger shook his head. He took a swallow of coffee and set the cup down on the rough table. "Not in a saloon. Drago found out from Sharon that I have some academic background in mining, and he came to me and asked if I'd be interested in managing his mining properties."

"Mining properties?" Molly asked in surprise.

Roger nodded. "I turned down a lot of money when I shook my head at him. Call it foolish pride — as Sharon does — but I won't work for the man who owns the table where I got skinned out of my money."

"You're talking about when you first came to Creede?" Molly asked.

"Yeah," Roger said with a pained expression. "I was a fool, and I've got nobody to blame but myself, but that was a crooked table in the Orleans Club. I found that out later when Sharon went to work for Drago. Don't get me wrong, Sharon deals a fair hand. She won't cheat anyone. But Drago pressures his dealers to cheat men who are cross-eyed drunk or green as grass. Put me

157

in that last category. I have a weakness for draw poker, not liquor." He added, "As you can guess, Sharon and I don't talk about Drago. She knows how I feel about him, and I know what she's after. I don't blame her. Truth is, a woman doesn't have much of a chance to hit it big around here. Everybody comes to Creede to make a fortune, and we're no different."

"I didn't know about any mining properties owned by Drago," Molly said. "He gave me the impression that he invests only in town property."

"That's probably true," Roger said, "but when a hard-luck miner puts shares of stock or a claim deed on the table in the Orleans Club, you can be sure Drago won't turn him away. That's how he has come to own a few mines. Most are nothing but tunnels blasted into country rock, but Drago probably got them for a dime on the dollar. He can turn around and sell them to some newcomer who wouldn't know silver from galena."

"You know where these mines are?" Molly asked.

Roger nodded. "I looked over a map Drago brought when he offered me the job. He wanted me to find out if any of them might have some promise. I could tell by the location that they didn't. There's a mineral belt here, and these were too far off of it. I told Drago as much."

"Can you point them out to me?" Molly asked.

Roger cast a surprised look at her. "I suppose I could. Why?"

"I haven't been able to locate Dave Hughes anywhere in town," Molly said. "Now I have another place to look."

"My God," Roger whispered, suddenly realizing the implication. "Do you expect to find him alive?"

"I don't know," Molly replied. "All I'm going on now is hope."

"I see," Roger said slowly as the gravity of this situation sank in. "I'll help in any way I can, but I don't know how Sharon will react to this."

"Perhaps we'd better keep this between the two of us for now," Molly said. "Then if I turn up some evidence, we can lay it out for Sharon and let her draw her own conclusions."

Roger considered that suggestion. He nodded agreement. "Now, what do you want me to do?"

After nightfall Molly returned to Creede Avenue. Greeted by the jumble of merry sounds from brass bands, pianos, and fiddles in the saloons and dance halls, she walked the crowded boardwalks in hopes she would find Dave. All the while she kept watch for Drago or any of his men.

The night hours passed and by midnight she had seen neither the man she wanted to avoid nor the one she desperately sought. Finally she went back to the Fifth Avenue Hotel. At the desk she made arrangements to have a saddle horse ready for her in the morning, and left instructions that under no circumstances was she to be disturbed tonight. If any visitors came, they should be asked to leave a message. She believed it was unlikely that Dave would come here, and she certainly wanted to prevent Drago from banging on her door tonight. Between the time she had escaped and this hour he might have discovered she was gone.

In her room, Molly got into bed and closed her eyes the moment her head sank into the pillow. The day had left her physically exhausted and emotionally drained. She did not open her eyes or even move until the wakeup call came at five in the morning.

The knock on her door brought her out of bed, instantly awake. She dressed hurriedly, putting on her divided riding skirt and boots, and after a quick breakfast she left the hotel. At the hitch rail outside was a chestnut mare from a nearby livery. Molly adjusted the stirrups, checked the saddle cinch, then swung up. She rode out of town on Creede Avenue, empty now, and headed for Willow Creek Canyon.

The canyon was still in deep shadow, but the sky overhead was bright with the morning sun. Molly followed the rutted freight road that followed the narrow-gauge railroad tracks into the mountains. She rode past the long boardinghouse. Back against the canyon wall she saw the cabin where Sharon Hughes was undoubtedly in bed now.

Ahead in Upper Creede, Molly saw a lone figure on the roadside. He waved as she drew near.

"Morning," Roger said.

Molly halted and took her foot out of the left stirrup. "Climb up," she said. "We'll ride double."

Dressed in work clothes and carrying his lunch pail, Roger grinned up at her. "Beats walking." He thrust his boot into the stirrup and swung up behind her.

Molly touched her heels to the mare, guiding the saddle horse along the road that passed between the unpainted buildings of Upper Creede. Beyond the settlement the road followed the winding course of Willow Creek in the floor of the canyon. A mill came into sight, perched on the steep side of the canyon wall, with tailings and settling ponds at the bottom. The mill used gravity in the process of reducing raw ore to a fine concentrate that was shipped out in railcars.

Above the mill Molly passed miners on the road. Like Roger, they carried lunch pails and were in the habit of walking to work every morning. For some that meant a two-hour hike before a full day's work blasting and hammering out rock and moving ore. At a fork in the road Molly drew rein. Roger swung a leg over the horse's rump and slid to the ground.

He gestured to the right, where a wagon road switchbacked up the side of the canyon wall. "Over the top you'll come to another branch in the road. Go left, and in a few miles you'll come to a fence and a stout gate with an unfriendly sign. That's Drago's property, stretching down into a little valley. He owns several mines down there, but the last I heard nobody's working them. Like I told you, there's a lot of prospect holes over in that district, but nobody's ever found anything but country rock."

Molly nodded. "Thanks. I can find my way from here."

Roger gazed up at her. "I don't feel right about sending you off like this, by yourself."

"I'm used to working alone," Molly said with a smile.

"You be careful," he went on. "Drago may have a guard or two up there to keep out claim jumpers. These mountains are crawling with fortune seekers."

"I'll keep an eye out," Molly said. "Thanks again for your help." She rode away, bearing to the right where the narrow road angled up the steep slope.

The mining road climbed the mountainside like the laces of a boot. It wound back and forth, one sharp turn after another, switchbacking up to the summit. As she gained elevation Molly looked down into the canyon bottom, seeing the creek and the road down there. The buildings of the mill grew small, and by the time she reached the top they looked like children's toys. A tiny train snaked into the canyon with black smoke drifting up toward her, and through the abyss she heard the engine's shrill whistle when it reached the end of steel at the mill.

Pines fringed the crest of the mountain. Molly entered the fragrant shadows of the trees, and came to the fork in the road Roger had described. She angled to the left.

This road was little used, and patches of

weeds and tufts of grass showed through the ruts left by iron-tired wagon wheels. It had evidently been constructed during the initial rush for silver, when hopes were highest. But hard-earned experience had proved that the mineral belt Roger talked about was on the other mountain, where he and hundreds of other men now worked deep underground. Fortunes had been made over there, and the promise of more drove men like Roger to work hard six days a week and go out prospecting on the seventh.

The mountaintop slanted down into a vast forest of pines and spruce mixed with aspen. Molly saw the sea of treetops when she rode out of the trees and entered the high side of a clearing. Straight ahead the wheel ruts led to the gate Roger had mentioned.

The pole gate was suspended between two stout posts and locked with a heavy chain and brass padlock. No fence stretched out from the gate, but slender lodgepole pines on either side were as thick as the hair on a dog's back. The dense forest was as effective as any fence. No ore wagon could pass through, and as Molly drew closer she saw that it would be a tight squeeze even for a horse.

On the gate she saw a sign nailed to the

top cross pole. Crudely painted, the letters were dimmed by weather and time. The words made a simple declaration, a threat of the kind she expected from Lou Drago:

KEEP OUT
TRESPASSERS WILL
BE SHOT

XV

Molly left the road and slowly entered the thick stand of trees beside the gate. She eased the saddle horse through a gap between two lodgepole pines, ducking down over the animal's neck as needled branches raked her shoulders and back. Seeing faint hoofprints in the soil here, she realized that other horsebackers had made this detour.

She came out of the trees on the road behind the gate, turned the horse, and followed the old mining road on its winding course down the sloping side of the mountain. Birds sang high in the trees, and overhead Molly saw a large hawk circling. The predator banked and effortlessly swooped away.

The road took a sharp turn, and fifty yards farther Molly drew rein as she entered a clearing. Abandoned mine buildings were here, steep-roofed structures behind a pile of oxidized tailings. Something about the dark windows and missing doors made the place seem sinister, even though Molly felt certain no one was here. She saw no fresh signs of horses, or anything else to indicate that anyone had been here recently.

But she did see something. Hoofprints on the road angled off into the trees. Molly followed them, and had ridden only a few yards when she caught the scent of wood smoke. She halted and swung down, tying the horse's reins to a branch.

Drawing her revolver, she moved cautiously through the forest, feeling brittle pine needles crunch beneath her boots. The trees became widely spaced, and ahead she saw more mine buildings. Smoke drifted out of a rusty stovepipe in the roof of a shack. The horse trail through the trees was evidently a shortcut from the road to these mine buildings.

Molly moved to her right, angling toward the shack, and a pair of horses came into view. Saddled but not bridled, they were tied behind the shack, switching their tails as they nosed into a hay manger. Molly knelt down behind a tree and waited.

More than half an hour had passed when she heard a door screech on rusted hinges. A bearded man came out carrying a bucket. Molly watched him move around the side of the shack to a heap of gray ashes and dump out the contents of the bucket. He stepped away from the cloud of dust and smoke that rose, then turned and went back inside.

Molly waited awhile longer before she moved in for a closer look. The wall of the shack she approached was windowless, the weathered and warped boards dotted with rusted nail heads. The horses lifted their heads and watched her, with their ears cocked, but neither animal whickered.

Molly moved to the wall of the shack. Just as she reached it, someone inside laughed. The coarse laughter brought on a fit of coughing, and then another voice came through the thin wall. Molly could not make out any of the words, but that second voice was vaguely familiar to her.

She went to the corner of the shack beyond the horses and looked around it. She saw a small window. Stepping carefully, she made no sound as she moved toward it. The four panes of glass reflected morning light. As soon as she saw that, she backed away. She could not see inside, and the danger of being seen was too great to risk a look.

Knowing she would either have to wait for something to happen, or make something happen, she retreated to the rear of the shack and stood by the horses. Then an idea came to her and she made her decision.

Molly walked to the pile of ashes on the other side of the hay manger. She held a hand over the gray ashes and felt heat radiating up. Turning, she scooped up an armload of hay and sprinkled it over the ashes.

Wisps of smoke drifted up for a few seconds, then began to billow. Molly added more hay. Flames leaped up. The horses rolled their eyes and reared, squealing.

Molly raced behind the cabin and ran to the front corner. Stopping there, she heard a curse. Boots pounded loudly on the board floor. The door banged open.

She glimpsed two men as they sprinted out and headed for the opposite side of the shack. The sight of fire brought shouts from them.

"What the hell —"

"Stomp it out!"

Molly moved quickly to the empty door, gun in hand. She stepped inside the crudely furnished shack. A table and a pair of bunks were there, a sheet-iron stove, and crates of canned food and supplies. On the floor near the back wall she saw an indistinct shape, rounded and dark. As she moved across the room, she saw that it was the body of a man. In the next moment she heard a protesting voice behind her.

"I tell you, I never throwed no hay on them ashes —"

"Well, if you didn't, who the hell did?"

Molly turned around and faced the doorway. The bearded man entered first, gazing over his shoulder toward his accuser. The moment the second man appeared, Molly recognized him. He was Drago's man, Sammy, still wearing the same dark blue suit and bowler hat he had worn when he'd followed her.

The pair came all the way inside before they saw Molly standing in the middle of the room with her gun aimed at them. They stopped short, mouths open.

"Lay down on the floor, spread-eagle," Molly said. "Both of you."

The bearded man drew a ragged breath and broke into a fit of coughing that racked his body.

"I thought Lou . . ." Sammy's voice trailed off.

"You thought Drago had taken care of me?" Molly asked with a smile. "Let's put it this way. He tried his best. Now do as I said."

When the two men only stared at her, Molly raised the barrel of her .38 and fired a shot past Sammy's ear. The bearded man gasped and coughed and dropped to the floor like a sack of flour. Sammy glowered at Molly, but slowly complied. He went to his knees and lay face down on the board floor.

"Spread-eagle, like I told you," Molly said. After they spread out their arms and legs, Molly searched them. Sammy carried a revolver in his waistband, but the other man was unarmed.

Holding her gun on them, Molly backed to the corner of the room and knelt beside the prone figure. She looked down at him. Horribly beaten, his eyes were swollen shut and dried blood caked his lips and jaw. His wrists were bound with wire.

Even so, Molly recognized him. Now she heard his shallow breathing. She reached out and gently touched his battered face. "Dave, can you hear me? Dave?"

He moaned. His head moved slightly.

"All right," Molly said softly. "Don't try to move just now. I'm going to get you out of here."

She stood and returned to the middle of the room. Looking down at the two men, she said, "You're a couple of heroes, aren't you? You tie a man's hands, then you take turns beating him."

The bearded man coughed. "Look, lady, I never did nothing. I never laid a hand —"

"Shut up," Sammy said in a low voice.

"You're the one who needs to shut up," Molly said, kicking his outstretched foot. "When I want to hear from you, I'll tell

171

you." Her gaze went to the corner of the room. She saw a spool of wire and a pair of pliers.

She went over there and unwound enough wire to bind the hands and feet of both men. She cut it into two-foot lengths, and first tied up Sammy and then bound the wrists and ankles of the bearded man. His protests were interrupted with coughs.

"Lady, I ain't well . . . don't hurt . . . me."

Molly went to Dave and used the cutters on the pliers to free his hands and feet. She helped him sit up, then got a bucket of water and found a towel near the stove. She washed his wounds while he leaned against the wall, head tipped back. He tried to speak through swollen lips.

"Shhhh," Molly whispered. But he continued trying to speak. Molly said, "Who did this to you — both of these men?"

Dave nodded. He raised a hand and gestured toward the sheet-iron stove.

Molly looked over there. Firewood and kindling were in a box beside it. One gnarled piece of stovewood was dark on one end. Molly realized it was darkened with blood.

"They beat you with that?" Molly asked.

Dave nodded again.

The bearded man whimpered and coughed wetly.

"Both men?" Molly asked again.

Dave nodded emphatically, his swollen eyes watering either from pain or from rage.

Molly's jaw set. "I want to get you out of here. Can you stand?"

Dave leaned forward and tried to get his feet under him. Molly stood and took his arm. She pulled, and he was able to come up to a crouching position. But when he tried to straighten up, he moaned against the pain.

Molly looked angrily at the two men on the floor. "You weren't satisfied to beat his face in," she said, "you had to kick him, too, didn't you? Didn't you?"

The bearded man said, "He wouldn't tell us —"

"Shut up!" Sammy said.

"Wouldn't tell you what?" Molly asked.

Around a wet cough the bearded man said, "Nothing. He wouldn't tell us nothing."

"I'll find out from Dave," Molly said. She helped him as he made his way across the room toward the door, each step a struggle.

"Hey, lady, you ain't gonna leave us here!" the bearded man said after her. "You can't leave us!"

"I can," Molly said, "and I am."

"We'll die!" he said, coughing.

"Could be," Molly said. "Depends on how long it takes for a lawman to come up here and pick you up. Maybe a bear will wander into this shack before that." Reaching the door, she pitched the pliers far down the sloping hillside in front of the shack. Then she helped Dave outside.

They made their way around the board shack, past the pile of disturbed ashes, and slowly walked to the horses. Dave grasped the saddle horn of the nearest one while Molly turned the other horse loose. She gave the animal a slap and it galloped off into the trees.

Molly found a bridle and put it on the remaining horse, working the bit into his mouth. After tightening the saddle cinch, she helped Dave mount up. This was a painful experience for him, first raising his booted foot high enough to reach the stirrup. Then Molly grasped his other foot and hoisted him up. Dave groaned with pain as his leg went over the horse's back and he settled gingerly into the saddle.

Molly took the reins and led the horse upslope into the forest. She found her horse where she'd left him. After untying the reins from the pine branch, she swung up. She turned the horse and rode away, leading the second horse. Dave rode hunched over, sweat streaming from his battered face, and he gripped the saddle horn with both hands.

Molly reached the weed-grown road and

followed it back to the gate. She guided her horse off the road and led Dave's through the dense stand of lodgepole pines. She ducked down and moved slowly ahead, looking back at the gambler, who leaned over the neck of his horse. After clearing the trees, she rejoined the road on the other side of the locked gate.

She rode on to the crest of the mountain and the road that angled sharply down the far side, all the while wondering what to do now. Not until she was descending the mountain on the switchback road did an answer come to her, one that just might solve the problem posed by Saul Philips.

She would go to Marshal John Light and lodge a charge of false imprisonment against Drago. She would also tell him of Drago's men she had left bound in the shack. That way, she would find out if Light was an honest lawman or just another of Drago's employees.

But the immediate question was what to do with Dave. He needed a doctor. It wouldn't be safe, though, to take him back to Creede. Her gaze went down the steep mountainside to the bottom of Willow Creek Canyon. The creek looked like shining silver from here, as it wound down to the buildings of Upper Creede. Then Molly realized there was only one place to go.

XVI

Molly reached the cabin shortly after noon. She rode to the door, dropped the reins of the following horse, and dismounted. Her knock on the plank door was answered by Sharon. Surprised, the young woman looked first at Molly. Then she saw the man hunched over the neck of the second saddle horse.

"He needs help," Molly said.

"Who . . ." Sharon's voice faltered. "Who is he?"

"Your father," Molly replied.

"Oh, no," Sharon whispered.

"Help me with him," Molly said. She turned and moved back to the horse's side. Sharon paused, then followed.

The two women lifted Dave down from the saddle. Each taking an arm, they steadied him as he walked stiff-legged into the cabin. They helped him cross the room and eased him onto the bed.

Dave lay back, gasping through swollen lips. Molly looked at Sharon. Tears streamed down her cheeks.

"I'll get a doctor," Molly said. "Is there

one in Upper Creede?"

Sharon absently shook her head while staring down at her father. "Doc Simms . . . on Wall Street . . ."

"All right," Molly said. "I'll send him up here." She turned away and hurried toward the door.

Just as she opened it, Sharon sobbed and called after her, "Molly, who did this?"

Molly stopped on the threshold and looked back, seeing a crying girl there, not a composed woman.

"Drago's men," she said, and left.

Molly rode fast down the canyon to Creede Avenue. Making her way through heavy midday horse-and-wagon traffic, she turned left on Wall Street. Beyond the Fifth Avenue Hotel she saw a small office building that until now had escaped her notice. A sign on the front door read: JACOB R. SIMMS, PHYSICIAN.

She found the doctor to be a short, dumpy man with a wide scar running down the side of his jaw. He was hardly the image of a physician, and Molly must have stared after he greeted her.

"Yes, yes," he said impatiently, "what sort of medical treatment do you need?"

"It's not for me," Molly said. "A man has been severely beaten. He needs attention right away."

Doctor Simms cast a look at her that revealed his suspicion. "He is your husband? A relative?"

Molly shook her head. "A friend. His daughter is with him right now in Upper Creede." She described the cabin next door to the long boardinghouse there.

"Yes, I know of the place," Simms said. "If he is as severely beaten as you say, this man will need extensive treatment." He paused.

Molly caught his meaning and felt a wave of anger surge through her. "My friend is not indigent, doctor. He'll pay cash for your services."

"Possibly so," Simms said, still making no move to pick up his bag and head for Upper Creede.

Molly opened her handbag and dug out a twenty-dollar gold piece. She thrust it out to him. "Here, this ought to cover your initial examination."

Simms did not smile or thank her, but calmly pocketed the coin. Then he pulled his coat off a tree by the door and shouldered into it. "Your indignation is understandable, miss," he said, "but I hope you understand my position. I receive many pleas for help like yours, usually late at night. For these I am rarely paid a cent, only elaborate promises." He gestured to the scar on his face. "And this town is a dangerous one, miss, very dangerous."

"I see," Molly said. She added, "I'm sorry."

Simms brushed away the moment of conflict with a wave of his hand. Then he snatched up his black bag and rushed out the door.

From the physician's office, Molly returned the saddle horse to the livery and then walked the length of Creede Avenue to the city marshal's office. The office was at one end of the county courthouse. Molly had spotted it the day she had gone there to check the list of names registered on marriage licenses.

John Light was not in when she arrived at the lawman's office, but Molly didn't go out looking for him. As far as she knew, she had not yet been seen by Lou Drago or any of his men, but she didn't want to press her luck. She waited inside the empty office by the window. Three-quarters of an hour later she saw the lanky peace officer round the corner at Creede Avenue.

Molly introduced herself when he entered, and watched his face to see how he reacted. She saw no sign of recognition, no indication that Drago had put him onto her. He simply studied her as any lawman would study an investigator.

Light's face, long and angular, did not reveal his private thoughts. His pale blue eyes regarded her while he leaned back against a corner of his desk, his low-slung holster snug to his thigh, and he brushed a hand across his fine handlebar mustache.

"Fenton operative," he said, nodding slowly. "Never would have guessed, a looker like you." He gazed thoughtfully at her for another long moment and asked, "What can I do for you?"

Molly gave a brief explanation of her investigation of Lou Drago's property holdings, then told of her abduction off the street and imprisonment in the storeroom of the Second Chance Saloon.

"He not only kidnapped me," Molly said, "but he threatened my life if I didn't leave town."

John Light said dispassionately, "You seem to be all right."

"That's because I've stayed out of sight until today," Molly said.

"Doing what?" Marshall Light asked.

Molly paused. "Marshal, I get the feeling you doubt the truth of what I've told you."

He did not answer immediately but continued looking at her with his ice-blue eyes. "My experience as a lawman tells me there are two sides to every story, Miss Owens. I want to hear Lou Drago's side of it." He stood. "If you'll wait here, I'll fetch him."

Molly watched him leave. She moved to the window and saw the tall lawman angle across the street, heading for Creede Avenue. She had withheld mention of her encounter with Drago's men at the mine shack. Now was not the time to put all her cards on the table, and she believed that in a few minutes she would have a much better idea where the lawman stood.

In less than ten minutes John Light came back. Lou Drago was at his side, his legs moving furiously to keep up with the stride of the taller man.

"Yeah, marshal," Drago said the moment he entered the office, "that's her."

Light said to Molly, "Lou tells me you've been harassing him, prying into his private affairs."

"I've done nothing illegal," Molly said. "I conducted an investigation that was open and aboveboard."

"The hell," Drago said. "She's nothing but a hired spy. Don't I have the right to keep my business private? Ain't this a free country?"

John Light nodded agreement.

"In a free country," Molly said, "no one

has the right to kidnap and imprison anyone else."

"What're you talking about?" Drago demanded.

"Marshal Light knows," Molly said, turning to him.

The lawman raised a hand to his mustache. He stroked it before he spoke. "Lou tells me he never locked you up in the Second Chance storeroom or anywhere else."

"So it's his word against mine," Molly said.

Light nodded slowly. "Appears so."

She saw a triumphant, challenging expression on Drago's face. She turned her gaze back to John Light. "Whose word do you believe?" Molly asked.

"The question is," he said, "can you prove the charges you're making against Lou?"

Molly shook her head. "No, I suppose I can't."

"I'm the one who oughta press charges," Drago said indignantly. "This woman won't leave me alone. She follows me everywhere, like a damned hound. I have a right to know who hired her, don't I, marshal?"

"Who did send you to Creede?" Light asked mildly.

"I'm not at liberty to give out any names," Molly said. She added, "As a lawman, you must know that."

Light did not acknowledge the point. Instead he asked, "Is your business in Creede finished?"

"Not quite," Molly said.

"I believe it is, Miss Owens," he said. "You've made enough trouble for one of our citizens. I'll be at the depot when the morning train leaves. I hope to see you board it." He held his cold gaze on her. "If you aren't, I'll come after you and you'll find yourself in a jail cell. Do you understand?"

"I understand perfectly, marshal," Molly said.

"Good," he said. "Now, I suggest you go get yourself a train ticket." He went to the door and opened it for her.

Molly left without a word, and as the door closed behind her she heard a deep chuckle of laughter. John Light was Drago's man, Molly now realized, but did she have the proof that would bring Saul Philips down here? With a backward glance, she turned left on Creede Avenue and walked out of town and into the mouth of Willow Creek Canyon.

The long boardinghouse and other buildings of Upper Creede were in sight ahead when she saw a black-topped buggy coming toward her. Moments later she recognized the driver and raised her hand.

Dr. Jacob Simms pulled back on the reins and drew the small buggy to a halt. Molly moved to the side of the vehicle and looked in at the round-faced physician.

"How badly hurt is he, doctor?" Molly asked.

"Internally," he said, "it's hard to say. He has broken ribs, of course, but he's not passing blood. From that, I take a measure of hope."

Simms paused. "His face isn't as seriously injured as one might think. His eyes appear to be normal under all that swelling. At first I thought his jaw was fractured, but upon further examination I changed my mind and now think the bone is all right." He added, "He's trying to talk now. That's a good sign."

Molly nodded. "Thank you for seeing him, doctor."

A trace of a smile crossed his lips. "I'll be coming back tomorrow, and probably for the next several days." That remark came almost as a concession, and he went on, "He must be a good man to command both the loyalty of a beautiful woman like you and the devotion of his daughter. As a matter of fact, I'd say he's a very lucky man indeed."

Molly smiled and stepped back as Dr. Simms took up the reins and urged the horse away. She realized he wanted to make up for his gruff manner when they had first met. Interesting, she thought, that in Sharon he had seen a devoted daughter. She thought about that as she hurried on to the cabin.

Sharon answered the door and let Molly in. "He's asleep," she whispered. "Doc Simms gave him morphine to take the pain away."

Molly moved across the room with her, looking at the still figure on the bed. Dave lay under the blankets now, his bruised and bloodied face in repose.

"Tell me everything," Sharon said in a low voice. "I want to know everything that happened."

"Only Dave can tell us everything," Molly said. She went on to explain how she had discovered him at the mine shack on Drago's property.

"Sammy," Sharon repeated. "I know him. He's in the Orleans Club all the time, watching for cardsharps." She paused, her lips pursed. "I should be getting dressed for work, but now I don't want to go. I was wrong about Lou. Or I didn't want to believe the truth. Maybe I knew it deep down. He's a ruthless man, but Creede is filled with ruthless men and only the tough and smart ones survive." She had spoken with a clenched jaw and now tears came to her eyes.

"Sharon," Molly said, "I may be the one who led Drago to your father. I didn't know it at the time, but Drago had put Sammy on my trail. That's probably how he made the connection between me and your father. Believe me, Drago isn't going to get away —"

Sharon was suddenly racked by sobs, and she waved a hand at Molly to stop. "No! No! I did it! I told . . . I told Lou that a professional gambler was setting him up. I'm the one who pointed daddy out to him."

XVII

Molly tried to comfort the sobbing young woman, but Sharon would not be consoled until she had confessed everything.

"I was so mad at daddy," she said. "He was ruining my plans and he wouldn't leave. I just wanted him to get out of Creede and leave me alone." She wiped her reddened eyes. "So I told Lou that I'd recognized a professional gambler posing as a working man. The next time I saw daddy I pointed him out to Lou. I thought . . . I thought . . . oh, I don't know what I thought." She began crying again.

"But you didn't tell him Dave is your father," Molly said.

"No, of course not," Sharon said. "I didn't want anything to do with daddy until you brought him here." She looked at Molly. "The moment I saw him hunched over that horse I knew what a terrible thing I'd done. Molly, I'm no good. As soon as daddy's well, I'm going to leave and no one will ever see me again —"

Molly reached out and took her hand.

The hand was hot and damp. "You've made a mistake — a big one. But you've seen it for what it is. That proves to me that you're an honest person, Sharon. You're just fallible like the rest of us."

She said hoarsely, "I feel so bad, so damned bad."

Molly squeezed her hand. "I have an idea that might make you feel better."

"What?" Sharon asked.

"I'm convinced Lou Drago has committed worse crimes than having a man beaten within an inch of his life," Molly said. "I want him brought to justice."

Sharon gazed at her, blinking.

"To do it," Molly said, "I'll need your help. When you go to the Orleans Club this afternoon —"

"I can't go back there — ever," Sharon interrupted. "I never want to see Lou or Sammy or any of them again."

"You must," Molly said. "I need you."

"For what?" Sharon asked.

"To keep your eyes and ears open," Molly replied. "Drago has no suspicion toward you. You're in a position to find out things that no one else can."

Sharon drew a deep breath. She closed her eyes and shook her head.

Molly released her hand. "You're right."

Sharon's eyes opened. "What do you mean?"

"I have no right to ask you to spy on Drago," Molly said. "You'd be putting your own life in danger —"

"It isn't that," Sharon broke in. "I'm not afraid. It's just that I can't stand the idea of working for Lou after what he did. . . ." Her voice trailed off and she added, "No, I'm not afraid."

Molly watched as her gaze went across the room to the still figure of her father on the bed. When she again looked at Molly, her expression had hardened.

"Wait," she said softly. "I can do this. I can do it for daddy. I can make sure Lou Drago never harms anyone else."

Molly grinned.

Caught up in sudden enthusiasm, Sharon said, "Yes, I'll do it!"

"Just remember," Molly said, "we're gathering evidence, not taking the law into our own hands."

Sharon nodded vigorously, but then her expression grew troubled. "It won't do any good to turn evidence over to Marshal Light."

"I know," Molly said. "He won't know what's happening until it's too late. I'm in communication with a United States marshal in Denver. Everything we turn up goes directly to him."

Sharon considered that, and said, "Denver is a long ways from here, Molly."

"If we can make a convincing case," she said, "that U.S. marshal will be on the next southbound train."

"I see," Sharon said. "So it's up to us to make that case."

"That's right," Molly said with a smile. "You and me."

Sharon said, "I feel like I ought to apologize to you, Molly. I acted ugly toward you when you were only trying to help me."

"No need to apologize," Molly said. "That's in the past."

"For what it's worth," Sharon said, "I liked you from the first. You're a woman who gets things done. That's what I want to be, even though it's a man's world out there." She added, "I'm glad we're working together now."

"Me too," Molly said.

"Tell me where to start," Sharon said, leaning forward.

"You start by not doing anything out of the ordinary," Molly said. "Drago is a shrewd man, and if he suspects you're up to something, he'll react violently."

"But if I don't do anything —" Sharon began.

"Leave it to me," Molly said. "I'm in a position to make things happen. You're in a position to watch and listen. Understand?"

Sharon nodded reluctantly.

"When the time comes for you to take action," Molly said, "we'll both know it. But for the time being you must be very careful not to raise any suspicions."

"All right," Sharon said.

Long after Sharon had dressed and left for work at the Orleans Club, Molly sat at the rough pine table, thinking. Doubts crowded into her mind. Trouble lay ahead. She sensed it, and knew it could come from several directions. Both Drago and Light were hot on her trail now and she would have her hands full fending them off.

She hoped she had convinced Sharon of the necessity of not drawing attention to herself. If anything happened to the young woman, the responsibility would fall on Molly. . . .

Her dark thoughts were interrupted by footfalls outside. The door opened slowly. She reached into her handbag, fingers closing around the grips of her revolver.

Roger Hall looked in, his eyes wide with surprise. He opened the door all the way and came in. "Saw a lamp burning and wondered who was here."

His gaze swept across the room to the bed. He swore softly. He went to the bed and looked down at Dave Hughes.

"We've had some trouble," Molly said.

Roger turned to face her. "What happened?" He took off his hat and coat and hung them from a peg in the log wall, then pulled off his muddy boots. He crossed the room to the table.

Molly told him about the men she had encountered in the mine shack and her discovery of Dave Hughes. "Sammy and that other man were trying to get information out of him. I don't know what. I'm hoping Dave will be able to tell us that in the morning."

Roger looked across the room at him. He said in a low voice, "My God, he looks bad."

"Dr. Simms says he'll recover," Molly said.

"How did Sharon take it?"

"She's very upset," Molly said, "and feels guilty."

"Why?" Roger asked.

"I'd better let her tell you," Molly said.

"She's somehow responsible?" Roger asked.

Molly nodded.

"Then she must have identified her father

to Drago," Roger said. "Damn!"

Molly was impressed by his shrewdness. She explained that the betrayal was now the reason behind Sharon's eagerness to help in the investigation of Lou Drago.

"Well," Roger said, exhaling tiredly, "I understand how she must feel, but I don't like that. I don't like it one bit."

"She won't be taking an active part," Molly said. "All I've asked her to do is keep her eyes and ears open. Drago trusts her, and I certainly don't want her to do anything to break that trust."

Roger frowned and shook his head. "You don't know Sharon. She's likely to start her own investigation."

"I talked to her about how important it is not to do that," Molly said. "Roger, I think this experience has changed her outlook on life — changed it a great deal."

"Maybe," he said.

Molly heard the doubt in his voice. She understood his concern. Drago had proved himself to be a man of violence and Roger knew Sharon to be a strong-willed, impetuous woman. She had acted brashly before and he believed she would again, this time endangering her own life.

Molly hoped he was wrong. And she was determined to act rapidly to bring her investigation to a head, not giving Sharon time to get into trouble.

After supper Molly stretched out on blankets Roger spread on the floor. She napped for more than an hour. When she awoke the cabin was dark and silent but for Dave's light snoring. Roger had evidently gone out to a saloon. Molly left the cabin and walked down the black canyon to Creede Avenue.

The street was teeming with men and a scattering of women, most of whom were seeking business. From the second-story windows overlooking the boardwalks, other prostitutes called out to the men below, their beckoning voices strangely musical and sweet in the night. Harsher sounds of raw-voiced saloon barkers and brass bands came from the open doorways of the busiest saloons.

Molly made her way through the flowing crowds, ignoring the stares of lonely men and the whistles and shouted questions from the bolder ones among them. Then her eyes briefly met the angry gaze of Calamity Jane. The big woman swept past without a word. Molly glanced back in time to see her barge through the door of a gambling parlor, disappearing inside.

She left the cacophony behind as she turned right on an empty side street and walked hurriedly through the darkness toward the glowing windows of the train depot. Inside at the screened telegrapher's window Molly sent two messages. One was wired to Horace Fenton in New York. The second went to the United States marshal's office in Denver, addressed to Saul Philips.

Molly left the quiet depot and walked back to Creede Avenue and the center of town. Someone was drunkenly reciting a poem recently written about this camp, loudly shouting the refrain: "It's day all day in the daytime. And there is no night in Creede."

She crossed the rutted street and followed the boardwalk to the Orleans Club. She entered, her eyes sweeping across the crowd of men wearing bowler hats or wide-brimmed felt hats, their voices making a low roar of sound amid thick cigar smoke drifting toward the high ceiling in a steady blue haze. Lou Drago was not among them.

Molly went through the crowded saloon and stepped into the gambling parlor. The back room was crowded too, but not as loud. Men stood or sat around gaming tables, intently watching their fortunes rise and fall with the turn of a card or throw of the dice.

The largest group of men stood at the rear of the parlor, knotted around Sharon's twenty-one table. Molly glimpsed her down-turned face as she shuffled cards, but in the next moment her attention was caught by a pair of staring eyes. Molly turned and met the gaze of Roger Hall. He stood against the back wall, obviously having taken a position where he could watch over Sharon.

Molly did not look at him for long, and was considering what to do when she was jabbed in the back.

"Get out."

Molly turned around to see Lou Drago. Face reddened, he breathed hard, as though he'd been summoned and had come on the run. His outstretched index finger had just poked her in the back, and now he waved it at her.

"Get outa my club."

"That's not a very friendly way to treat someone who's bringing you a message," Molly said.

"You don't know nothing I wanta hear," he said. "You're making a disturbance. So get out, or I'll sic the law on you."

Molly smiled. "And your man wearing the badge will put me in a jail cell, is that it, Mr. Drago?"

"You don't believe me?" he asked.

"Oh, I believe you," Molly replied.

"So get out," Drago said.

"I'm on my way," Molly said, "after I tell you about your man, Sammy."

Drago's hand shot out and grasped her arm at the elbow. "There's nothing you can tell me about Sammy that I don't already know. I ain't worried about him." He added, "But you oughta be."

Molly saw the triumphant look on his face.

"I'm way ahead of you, detective lady," Drago said. "I know all about what happened up there at the mine, and I know you and that two-bit gambler are in this thing together." He gave her arm a yank. "Now get outa here!"

Molly did not resist as she was pulled unceremoniously through the archway dividing the gambling parlor from the saloon. Drago did not release her until he'd given her a last shove out the batwing doors.

Molly stumbled out to the boardwalk, aware that every man in the saloon stared after her in amazement. She caught her balance and moved away from the flapping doors. Anger flooded through her. She would have liked to have defended herself against Drago. She took a deep breath to calm herself.

Now Drago had connected her with Dave. She knew that much. And she knew Sammy was gunning for her.

XVIII

A group of loud-talking teamsters pushed through the batwing doors of the Orleans Club. Molly started to walk away, but turned back when her name was called. Roger came out. Without another word he moved to her side and they strode away, heading for the dark shadows of the nearest side street. They rounded the corner of the hotel next door to the club.

Roger stopped and faced her, his voice shaking when he spoke. "What were you trying to do in there? I couldn't help you without drawing attention to myself —"

"Roger," Molly said, "I can take care of myself. I am a professional investigator and I know what I'm doing. Right now, I don't need your help. In fact, you shouldn't be in that club at all."

"Just what do you mean by that?" he demanded.

"Now, cool down," Molly said. "Think about it. Drago knows you, doesn't he?"

"I suppose he remembers me," Roger said. "But he doesn't know about Sharon and me."

Molly asked, "You don't normally hang around in the Orleans Club, do you?"

"I know what you're getting at," Roger said. "Drago will be suspicious of me."

"He's shrewd," Molly said. "Anything out of the ordinary will catch his attention."

"So by trying to protect Sharon," he said, "I might have been endangering her."

"That's right," Molly said.

Roger drew a deep breath and exhaled loudly.

"I'm not questioning your motives, Roger," she went on, "just your methods. I want to protect Sharon, too."

"You're right," he said. "I wasn't thinking." He paused. "Well, what's your plan?"

"It's best I keep that to myself," Molly replied. "But don't worry, I've set things in motion. Drago won't be able to get comfortable as long as I'm in this town."

Roger laughed softly, but then paused. "Damn, I'm sorry, Molly —"

"No harm done," she said.

"I hope," he said. "By the way, I saw Doc Simms a while ago. He said he was headed for Upper Creede tonight, and on his way back he'd check in on Dave. I reckon one of us ought to be there."

Molly took his arm. "Let's both go."

No moon was in the sky, and when they

walked along the freight road beside the gurgling creek that wound its way through the canyon, Molly felt as though they were deep underground, deep inside a tunnel, walking to nowhere.

In truth she did not have a plan now. The fact that Drago had found Sammy in the mine shack had caught her by surprise. Perhaps it should not have. She should have guessed. Drago was not a man to leave things to chance, and when Sammy had not returned to Creede, Drago had probably sent someone to find out why, or ridden up there himself.

The details did not matter now. The point was that Drago had been able to connect her with the gambler. He felt triumphant because he had snatched Dave out of Creede and administered punishment. Now he would expel Molly from this camp.

As she walked through the inky darkness at Roger's side, she considered what to do next. Drago had been right when he'd boasted that he was way ahead of her. Somehow Molly would have to catch up.

Ahead the pale lights of Upper Creede came into view. Curtained windows in the long boardinghouse glowed yellow with the light of kerosene lamps. In the cabin they found Dave just as they had left him, in a deep sleep. Molly held a lamp over him. She and Roger stood at his bedside and looked down at his bruised, swollen face, a handsome face that would bear scars now. Then a knock came at the door.

Molly turned and watched Roger cross the room and open the door. She expected to hear the voice of Dr. Simms, but instead a woman cursed, driving Roger back by the sheer power of her rage. She barged in, jaw jutting, hands lashing out.

"What in hell's going on here? Who're you, buster?"

"Lady, I —"

Calamity Jane drew back her arm, folding her hand into a fist. Molly saw what was coming, but couldn't move fast enough to stop the attack. Roger was too surprised to avoid it. He stared while the big woman's fist came around in a wild haymaker, smashing into his jaw. His head snapped around. For a moment he stood still, then his knees buckled and he sank to the plank floor.

Calamity Jane whirled, facing Molly. "You're next! Come on! I ain't afraid of you!"

"Jane," Molly said, "listen to me —"

"Listen, hell!" she bellowed. "I've got eyes. I follered you and this yahoo up here and I was a-looking in that window when you two was standing over Dave . . . oh, poor Dave . . . my God, look at him . . . what in the name of hell have you done to my man? Damn you, woman —"

"Jane!" Molly shouted. "Calm down and listen to me!"

"You lying bitch," Calamity Jane said, "I ain't gonna listen to you for a minute. I'm taking Dave out of here —"

"No, you aren't," Molly said.

Calamity Jane looked from her to Dave and back again. Her cheeks were flushed with rage as she stood there in the middle of the cabin, fists clenched, feet spread wide. On the floor behind her, Roger moaned.

Calamity Jane's face went slack. That sound seemed to bring the big woman to her senses for the moment. "What's going on here, Molly? That's all I want to know. Just what in hell is going on?"

"Hold on a minute, Jane, and I'll tell you the whole story." Molly moved past her and knelt beside Roger. His eyes fluttered and he tried to sit up.

"Easy now," Molly said. Grasping his arm, she helped him stand. He was still dazed and his legs were rubbery. Molly helped him into a chair at the table and saw that his eyes were beginning to clear.

"What happened?" he asked in a blurred voice.

Across the room Molly heard a loud sob. She saw Calamity Jane standing over the bed, crying hard as she looked down at the sleeping Dave Hughes.

"Dammit, Molly," she cried out, "how did this happen?"

Molly judged the second question to be the most urgent. She left Roger and went to Calamity Jane's side, seeing her tear-stained cheeks and quivering lips.

By the time Dr. Simms arrived, Molly had completed her account of the events that had led to her discovery of Dave Hughes in the mining shack. Calamity Jane listened intently, eyes widening when Molly identified herself as a Fenton operative. While Molly did not relate every detail, she did give the highlights of her investigation.

Calamity Jane stood at the foot of the bed while Dr. Simms made a brief examination of Dave's wounds. She didn't say a word, but was clearly relieved to hear the physician express his belief that Dave would be all right and should be wide awake tomorrow. Simms then departed, saying he would return in twenty-four hours.

"So you're a Fenton detective, and you've

been working for Dave all this time?" Calamity Jane asked as soon as the door closed behind the doctor.

"That's right," Molly said. She crossed the room to the kitchen table, where Roger sat. Molly had poured him a cup of coffee and the brew had cleared his head. He cast a wary look at Calamity Jane.

"Look, I'm sorry I banged you like I done," she said. "I thought . . . well, I figured you had done something to Dave, that's all, and I lost my head."

"I nearly lost mine, too," Roger said, rubbing his jaw. "You hit hard."

"You feeling all right?" Molly asked.

Roger nodded slowly. "My pride's hurt. I've never been hit by a woman, much less floored by one."

"No call to rub it in," Calamity Jane said, irritated. "I told you I was sorry, didn't I? I never meant to do it."

Roger looked up at her. "I'm glad you weren't trying your hardest."

"Just so there's no hard feelings," Calamity Jane said. "I hate it when folks are mad at me. I've got enough troubles without that." She went on, "Let me get this straight now. You're married to Sharon? I declare. I knew her when she was just a little thing. Course, both Dave and me was younger back then — a lot younger."

Calamity Jane turned to Molly. "Well, you just gonna stand here and let that yahoo Drago get away with what he done to Dave?"

Molly smiled at the note of challenge in her voice. "I think you know me better than that, Jane."

"Figured as much," she replied. "You know, I'm not as dumb as folks take me for. I figured you've got some scheme cooked up, something you and Dave worked out."

That was close enough to the truth, and Molly nodded in reply.

"Figured as much," Calamity Jane said again. "And I figure you don't want my help. You want me to stay out of the road."

Molly said, "If I need your help, I'll come looking for you."

"Yeah," Calamity Jane said. She paused, turning to look at Dave. "Well, there's only one thing I want."

"What?" Molly asked.

"I want to come a-visiting," she said. "I want to look in on Dave without having to fight to do it."

Molly nodded slowly. "I believe we can arrange that."

"Well, good," Calamity Jane said. Her eyes blinked rapidly. "I can't stand the idea of him being hurt." Tears rolled down her cheeks. She ducked her head and moved to the door. Blindly reaching for the latch, she yanked open the door. She left, leaving the door open behind her.

Roger's face showed a mixture of disbelief and relief when she was gone. "Now I know where they got the word *hurricane*. It's a swirling, dangerous storm, named for that woman."

Molly slept on the floor of the cabin that night, awakening when Sharon came in at four-thirty. The young woman was too keyed up to sleep. She wanted to know everything that had happened last night.

They sat in the darkness at the rough table while Molly quietly related the events. The two women talked quietly until daybreak, then stoked up a fire in the stove and made a breakfast of scrambled eggs, bacon, and hot biscuits.

Roger got up and ate with them. Sharon gave him a hug and commiserated with him when she saw the bruise on his jaw. He assured her that if the incident was never mentioned again, he would be happy to forget the whole thing. He pulled on his work boots, picked up the lunch bucket Sharon had filled, and left for work.

Molly and Sharon were cleaning up the

breakfast dishes half an hour later when Dave suddenly sat up in bed, looked at them, and uttered a single word through swollen lips.

"Hungry."

He was weak, but he gradually revived from his drugged sleep after eating four scrambled eggs and drinking a cup of fresh goat's milk that Sharon had purchased from an old man who lived in Upper Creede. Dave recalled his rescue, but the events of the thirty-six hours before that were lost to him. This blank space in his memory at first only frustrated him, but then he became increasingly angry as he attempted in vain to remember what had happened to him.

Before noon Dr. Simms came to the cabin. This time he questioned Dave while examining him, asking where he felt pain. Dave cried out when his ribs were probed. The large, ugly bruises on his buttocks and abdomen, however, were not terribly painful to him.

"That's a good sign," Simms concluded after peering into Dave's ears and eyes. "You've been kicked and punched, but apparently none of the blows did internal damage. You're not passing blood, either."

"Doc," Dave said, "I can't . . . I can't remember . . . what happened."

"That's to be expected," he said. "You've been worked over by experts, and you've taken several blows on the head. Don't worry. Limited memory loss is nothing to fear. Chances are it'll all come back to you."

"Chances are," Dave repeated. "When? I want to know when."

"I can't predict that," Simms replied as he returned his stethoscope to his bag. "Ten minutes or ten weeks from now. Sometime in between those two estimates, I suppose."

Dave shook his head, frowning. "I remember some bastard kicking me. . . ."

Molly said, "One of the men hit you with a piece of stovewood. You told me that much."

"Yes," Dave said slowly, "that's right. . . ."

"Everything will come back to you," Simms said again. He stood and moved toward the door. Molly and Sharon met him there.

"He'll recover," Dr. Simms confided, "but it will take time. Three or four weeks, I'd say. He has some cracked ribs, but none are dislocated. His breathing will be painful for a good long while." The physician opened the cabin door and added, "Keep him in bed as long as you possibly can. Rest is the best medicine now."

Sharon listened, her hands clasped under her chin, eyes downcast.

"That's good news, doctor," Molly said, when she saw that Sharon was unable to speak. "Thanks for coming."

"If any problems develop," he said, "such as passing blood, let me know right away." He went outside.

Sharon blurted, "I'll pay you. How much do we owe you?"

Simms replied with a shake of his head and a brief smile. "I've already been paid in full." He strode out to his buggy.

Sharon took a deep breath. "Such a kind, compassionate man."

"Yes, isn't he?" Molly said. She closed the cabin door.

Dave's mental struggle went on through most of the afternoon. He became increasingly irritable with both Sharon and Molly, and angry with himself. Then, half an hour after Sharon left for work, the dawning moment came.

"I remember!" he shouted, slapping a hand down on the quilt. "I remember!"

As Molly suspected, Dave Hughes had developed a plan to recover Sharon's money from Drago. He implemented his scheme by first losing several poker hands in parlors owned by Drago. Among the dealers he quickly earned a reputation as a hard-luck gambler, a sucker. After losing over one thousand dollars, he had produced a hat full of rich silver ore and a deed to a mine, suggesting that the stakes be raised.

Drago himself had to approve such a game, but when he was summoned he expressed considerable skepticism. While he seemed to accept Dave as another amateur poker player, he pointed out that he had no way of knowing whether or not the ore actually came from the mine Dave was offering. In the end, he declined a winner-take-all poker game.

Dave had anticipated this response and did not hurry the deal. Instead, he simply made a show of selling more silver ore and promptly lost the cash at a table in the Orleans Club. By this time the dealers were convinced.

"They were ready to move in for the kill,"

Dave told Molly, "and I knew they were working on Drago to set up a high-stakes game." He lay back on the pillow, his swollen eyes closed.

After a long silence he continued, speaking slowly. "But something went wrong. Somehow he got onto me. I was grabbed out of the boardinghouse where I had a room. Two men hauled me into the mountains — that same pair you got the drop on in the shack. They wanted to know what my game was . . . who I was working for."

Grimacing as he drew a breath, he said, "I don't know what happened . . . I was playing in other clubs, winning to pay for the show I was putting on for Drago's benefit. That's how I got that deed to a worthless mine — I won it from an old geezer who thought he was putting one over on me." He paused. "Maybe Drago found out the only poker hands I lost were in his clubs. Maybe that's how he got onto me."

Molly interrupted his speculation by asking, "Where did you get all that silver ore?"

"From a miner who was high-grading out of a tunnel in his lunch bucket," Dave replied. He looked at her. "If you're thinking he gave me away, forget it. He'd have been run out of the district if he breathed a word of it."

Dave's voice was drawn with fatigue. Presently he dozed, able to sleep now that he had recovered his memory.

Molly looked at his still face. She knew that a very painful time lay ahead when his daughter came home. Sharon would solve the mystery in Dave's mind. Hearing that confession of betrayal would hurt him even more, Molly suspected, than the beating he had taken at the hands of Drago's men.

Molly waited until Roger came in from his shift in the mine. Together they prepared supper, and she made venison broth for Dave. He sat up in bed and took it down one steaming spoonful at a time, watching enviously while Molly and Roger dined on venison steaks. Several of his teeth were loosened, and it would be quite a while before he would be able to eat food more substantial than soup or scrambled eggs.

Molly noted, however, that Dave was already regaining some of his strength. He was growing restless, even though a deep breath still wrenched his whole body and brought shining droplets of sweat to his forehead. By the time Molly was ready to leave the cabin, Roger was seated on the edge of the bed, watching the gambler shuffle a deck of cards in a way that kept a pair of aces on the bottom.

Dave demanded to know where she was going and what she planned to do. Molly gave him a smile and a good-bye wave, and left without telling him.

She walked through the cool, pale light of evening to Creede, a scarf wrapped over her head against the chilling breeze wafting out of Willow Creek Canyon. On the boardwalk of Creede Avenue she made her way through the jostling crowds. She kept her hand in her handbag, fingers wrapped around the grips of her revolver. From a street corner across the way came the booming oratory of Preacher Ed, warning sinners of the fiery fate that awaited them, that time was growing short.

Molly went on to Wall Street, where she turned left and hurried on to the Fifth Avenue Hotel, leaving the shouting and shoving crowd behind. She was much in need of a hot bath and a change of clothes. At the hotel desk she ordered the bath, then climbed the staircase to her room, feeling enough soreness in her muscles to remind her of last night's makeshift bed on the floor of the cabin. In her room she lit a lamp. The thick mattress on the bed looked very inviting.

It took all of her willpower not to succumb to temptation and lie down. She craved a good night's sleep. But she could not rid herself of the feeling that, as Preacher Ed had shouted to the masses, the end was near. One way or another, this case would soon be resolved. But how? And who would come out on top?

Molly thought about all the angles to this case while she was submerged in the tub of steaming water that had been brought into her room. She knew that if she lost control of the events she had set in motion, Sharon's life might be lost.

She must act tonight. She had to keep pressure on Lou Drago. If she failed to get the jump on him, she knew who else would try. Injured as he was, she doubted that Dave would stay in that bed more than another twenty-four hours.

Such disturbing thoughts prevented her from drowsing in the hot water surrounding her body. As heat seeped into her muscles, soreness seeped out. She stretched, enjoying this brief luxury.

At that moment she heard muffled sounds at the door. At first she thought someone had passed by in the hall, but then the soft sounds came again as someone or something brushed against the door. The handle rattled. Molly stood.

Just as she straightened up in the tub, water dripping from her body, the door opened with a tremendous bang, slamming against the wall. In the hall stood Marshal John Light, a sledgehammer in his hands. He stared at Molly, then grinned.

"Caught you."

Molly turned her back to him. "Get out!"

"No, I do believe I'll come in," Light said.

Molly shrieked.

"Scream all you want," Light said. "The management knows I'm here, and they know I'll buy 'em a new door."

Molly leaped out of the tub and lunged for the bed. Amid her pile of clothes there was the holstered derringer. . . .

But Light was too quick for her. Coming from behind, he thrust a boot under her feet and gave her a shove with the handle end of the sledgehammer. Molly went down, hitting the carpeted floor face first.

"Well, looky here," she heard him say, "a sneak gun."

Molly lay huddled on the floor while the lawman rummaged through her belongings, pulling the Colt .38 out of her handbag. Then he crossed the room and closed the door, the broken latch hanging askew.

"You're a fine-looking hunk of woman," he said, coming back to her. "Nice big butt, fine handsome shape to you. I ought to take my pleasure with you, right here and now."

Molly covered herself with her hands as

best she could. "You're no lawman. You're no better than the worst back-alley criminal in this town."

"Now that's no way for a woman in your position to talk to a man in my position," he said. He gazed down at her. "You had a chance to get out of Creede in one piece. For the life of me, I can't figure out why you're still here."

Molly spoke without looking at him. "I'm waiting."

"Waiting," he repeated. "For what?"

"A U.S. marshal is coming from Denver," Molly said. "I'm to meet him here."

"That so?" Light said mildly. "What's this feller's name?"

"Saul Philips," Molly replied.

"Never heard of him," Light said. "Lady, I do believe you're running a bluff, and I'm just the man to call you on it —"

"He's heard of you," Molly said.

"What're you talking about?" he said.

"You had some trouble down in Texas, didn't you?" Molly asked.

Light swore, then nudged her with the toe of his boot. "Get some clothes on."

Now Molly looked up at him. The man's face was red with anger.

"Move it," he said. "Or I'll drag you out of here just like you are."

"Where are you taking me?" Molly asked, not moving.

"From one hotel to another," he replied. He added, "To the one with bars on the windows."

"I want to dress in private," Molly said. "Then I'll go peaceably."

He grinned. "You'll go, peaceable or not. You're full of tricks, lady. So I'll just stand here and watch the show. Don't worry, I've seen nekkid women before. Stand 'em on their heads and they all look alike." He chuckled. "You're a whole hell of a lot safer with me than you'd be with Lou right now. Believe me. Good-looking woman like you. Lou has some different ideas, real different. So you'd better stick with me, lady."

Molly's skin grew hot. The man was enjoying this. He was doing everything short of rape to humiliate her. And from a certain gleam in his eyes she believed that would come later. She stood, trying to console herself by thinking that she would be ready for him, would give him a fight like he had never seen before.

Keeping her back to him, she slipped on her underclothes. Then she stepped into the clean dress she had laid out. All the while he stood half-a-dozen feet away, the sledgehammer in his hands. As she laced up her

217

shoes, she said, "There are better ways to come through a locked door, marshal."

He gazed down at her, obviously wondering why she was making conversation. He shrugged. "You're wrong about that. I reckon you can pick a lock, but I'll take a ten-pounder every time. See, if you'd had the door blocked, I'd have come right on through. Can't do that when you go to picking locks, can you?"

"No, I suppose not," she said, standing. She asked, "What about that murder charge down there in Texas? How did you beat it?"

Light's jaw set. "Drago was sure right about you. You just keep nosing around, don't you?"

"To tell you the truth," Molly replied, "I don't like the smell in here."

Setting down the sledgehammer, he swiftly moved toward her, drawing his Peacemaker. "Turn around, damn you."

Molly had intentionally angered him, hoping he would do something foolish. But now as she saw him pull handcuffs out of his hip pocket, she realized this was not the time to make her fight.

"Put your hands behind your back," he said, cocking the revolver. "Or are you gonna try to escape?"

Molly knew he was angry enough to pull that trigger. She turned around and clasped her hands behind her back. Cold steel was clamped on her wrists, and then she was yanked across the room and out the door.

Light pulled her down the staircase and half-dragged her through the lobby. They went out with hotel guests and bellmen staring after them.

Marshal John Light led Molly down the boardwalk along Wall Street to Creede Avenue. He shoved her into the middle of the street, and with several hundred men looking on he alternately dragged her and pushed her to the county courthouse at the far end of the camp.

Light pushed her into his office. He unlocked the rear door, grasped her arm and pulled her into the cellblock. "Back there," he said. "Move!"

Molly caught her balance when he gave her a rough shove, and made her way down the narrow aisle between the cells. There were half a dozen on either side. She had seen a number of town jails, dark and stinking cages where a few criminals and many drunks were housed, but this one was the worst she'd ever seen. Her nostrils filled with the stench of unwashed men, vomit, and urine. Light opened a cell door, then removed her handcuffs.

Molly stepped into the cell before the marshal could hit her or shove her again. He laughed, and slammed the barred door shut.

Long, silent minutes passed after he was gone. Molly's eyes adjusted to the gloom. She peered into the other cells, each eight or ten feet square, separated only by vertical steel bars. No wall or any other provision had been made for privacy between men and women prisoners.

"The answer to a dream . . . or my descent into hell?"

Startled, Molly looked toward the end cell, where the voice seemed to come from. Then she saw movement as a narrow-shouldered man stood.

"Alone with a beautiful woman," he went on, "a miserable captive like myself. Ah . . . but captivity will only enhance our physical pleasures . . . force us to live every minute to the fullest. What joys of the flesh are ours to savor!"

His voice rose, gaining power, and that was when Molly recognized it. He was the man who called himself Preacher Ed.

"But look," he said, dismayed, "even though we're here together, alone with our pleasures, we're separated by dark space . . . unable to touch. Ah . . . that is where my dream ends and my descent into hell be-gins."

Molly heard the man sob, and realized he

was drunk. She backed away from the cell door, momentarily glad that it was locked, and sat on the hard bunk attached by chains to the back wall.

"Won't even speak, will you?" Preacher Ed suddenly demanded. "No . . . you'll withhold your charms . . . your sweet and comforting voice . . . while I sink into the depths of hell . . . into the eternal flames. Angel of mercy? To me, you are an angel, yes. But to others, those brutes who walk the boardwalks, you're nothing but a whore."

After a long silence, Preacher Ed said angrily, "Isn't that right? Arrested for taking some poor bastard's money, weren't you? I know how you whores work . . . you stinking bitches . . . that's what you are, nothing but . . ."

Molly closed her eyes while his voice droned on. Presently the door to the marshal's office was flung open and the big lawman strode in, lantern in hand.

"Ed, shut up, will you? I can hear your damned howling clear out there in my office."

"Lock me up," Preacher Ed bellowed, "yes, you can lock up my physical being, but you'll never imprison my voice. Never! My voice is the trumpet of the fallen angel . . . heard by all you mortal sinners in the land —"

By the waving glow of the lamp Molly saw John Light draw back his fist. She saw swift movement, then heard a dull *thud* when the punch connected with Preacher Ed's jaw, silencing that voice. He quietly fell to the floor of his cell.

"Now maybe I can get some damned peace around here," Light said as he walked past Molly's cell. When he turned to close the door, he said to her, "Reckon you'll have a visitor afore long. Drago wants to have a talk with you." He pulled the door shut.

The cellblock sank into its musty gloom. The only sound now was a moan from Preacher Ed. Molly sat on the bunk, staring into the dim shadows. Time stood still.

She stretched out on the hard bunk for a time, but did not sleep, tired as she was. The stench made her feel ill, but even worse was the overwhelming sense of powerlessness she felt. She desperately wanted to know what was happening outside, yet her thoughts about it filled her with dread.

The hours of the night dragged past. Molly slept in fits and starts. Drago never came, and she wondered what had happened to keep him away. What did it mean? At daybreak she sat up, more depressed than ever. In hindsight she realized she should have fought Light in her hotel room. At least she had a slim chance there. Now she was at his mercy, under lock and key, with no hope of making a move against Drago.

The day passed. She saw only the face of a day deputy who brought a meal of watery stew and hard, moldy bread. Preacher Ed was subdued. He alternately lay on his bunk or sat on it, head bowed. His jaw was purple where he had been slugged. The few times his red-eyed gaze met Molly's through the bars, he gave no recognition. She wondered if he remembered his harangue or anything else that had happened last night.

By evening of that day Molly's mood was one of complete hopelessness. She would stay here as long as Drago wanted her to be imprisoned. He could leave her in this cell for weeks if he so decreed. This realization left her without hope, and turned her anger to a deep and dark depression.

But before nightfall help came in the most unexpected form. Molly heard a shrill voice through the door to the marshal's office, then a clash of bodies against the wall. A violent struggle was obviously going on in there. Moments later the door was thrown open.

"Molly! You in there? Answer me, dammit!"

Molly stood. The stout figure was backlighted, the face was darkened, and the lamplight from the office made a strange halo effect around the head. Hands perched on broad hips, legs spread — this was a pose Molly had seen before.

"Jane," she said, "I'm in here."

Calamity Jane charged toward her, a ring of skeleton keys in her hand. When she reached the cell door, she fumbled with the keys until she found the one that fit the lock.

"By God, I've always wanted to do this," Calamity Jane said excitedly. She straightened up and triumphantly flung open the barred door. Then she turned toward the other cells and shouted, "I'm letting ever' thief and beggar outta this hellhole. Get ready to celebrate, boys! You're free!"

Her call was met by silence. In the back cell, Preacher Ed stirred.

"Hell, there ain't but one other jailbird in here," Calamity Jane said, disappointed. She moved swiftly to the back cell. "What're you in here for, mister?"

Preacher Ed shrank away from her. He said nothing, but stared at her as though he were confronting the supernatural.

"Say," Calamity Jane said, "I know you, don't I? Sure I do. You're that preacher feller, ain't you?"

"Leave me be, lady," Preacher Ed whispered.

"What'd you do to get yourself locked up?" Calamity Jane asked. Without awaiting an answer, she bent down and thrust the key into his cell door.

"The sword of the Almighty will destroy this camp called Creede," Preacher Ed said, his voice rising.

"Well, get out there and spread the word," Calamity Jane said, throwing open the door.

"You are forgiven," Preacher Ed said, raising a hand in front of his face, "for you know not what you do."

"I know one thing," Calamity Jane said. "You've just been delivered by a sinner." She turned away from him. "Come on, Molly, let's get out of this stinkhole. Dave wants to see you."

XXI

Leaving the cellblock, Molly saw the prone figure of Marshal John Light on the office floor. Hands bound behind his back with handcuffs, he was gagged with a red bandanna handkerchief. He stared up at Molly, eyes bulging with rage.

"That lawdog gave me a hell of a tussle," Calamity Jane confided to Molly on their way through the office.

Molly turned and moved behind the marshal's desk. She opened the drawers and rummaged through them.

"Hey, we've got to get outta here," Calamity Jane said, standing nervously at the door. "No telling when a deputy will check in."

In a bottom drawer Molly found what she was looking for. She pulled out her Colt .38 and her derringer. Then she rushed out the front door a step behind Calamity Jane. They were followed, Molly noticed, by Preacher Ed, who ventured out of the office and then loped across the street, stovepipe hat in hand.

The heels of their high button shoes drummed on the planks of the boardwalk as they hurried to the intersection at Creede Avenue. Night was quickly falling. Evening shadows turned black. At the intersection they angled away from the raucous sounds of the mining camp and plunged into the cool darkness of Willow Creek Canyon.

Molly had to walk fast to keep pace with the long-legged stride of Calamity Jane. She was breathing hard by the time they reached the cabin. Inside, Dave and Roger were seated at the rough kitchen table, playing draw poker with two dummy hands. They both looked up when the door swung open, their expressions caught in a moment of utter surprise.

"Told you I'd bust her out," Calamity Jane said, "and by God, I done it. You owe me, Dave Hughes, damned if you don't."

For a long moment neither Dave nor Roger moved or spoke. Dave stared at Molly through blackened eyes, then his swollen lips spread into a broad smile.

Roger blurted, "How did you do it, Jane?"

Calamity Jane laughed in reply, obviously enjoying the moment.

Molly closed the cabin door and stepped into the room. "I'd like to know the answer to that myself."

Calamity Jane turned to her. "I saw that lawdog haul you off to the jailhouse. Well, I came up here right away and told these two jokers. You think either one of these grown men could think of anything to do about it? Hell no, they couldn't. They talked it over half the night, these two and Sharon. Talk, talk, talk, that's all men ever do. So finally I says, 'I'll go down there myself and bust that woman outta there.' You shoulda seen the look these two yahoos gave me."

She laughed again. "So that's what I done. 'Course, I had to get some shut-eye first. Then I had to pick my time, when Light was in that office alone. Couldn't do it during the day when a couple of deputies was sitting in there drinking coffee. Took him by surprise, I did. Got the drop on him and took his Peacemaker away from him. Then when he came at me, I used that big gun to bang him a good one on his hard head. Didn't knock him cold, but I sure as hell took the fight outta him. Oh, we had us a rassle there for a minute. Then I gagged him with his own dirty kerchief and pinned his hands behind his back with his own bracelets." She drew a deep breath. "Damn, but I wish that jail had been full of prisoners."

Calamity Jane turned to Dave. She beamed at him. "So I win our bet, don't I?"

The uncomfortable silence that followed brought a triumphant laugh from the big woman. She had made her point, and Dave's silence only served to acknowledge her victory. At last he did speak, his words blurred by swollen and scabbed lips.

"You have to get out of here, Jane," he said.

The smile faded from her face. "What're you talking about?"

"I'm talking about keeping you alive," he said. "You won't be if you don't get out of Creede — tonight."

"Now, hold your damned horses," she said, advancing a step toward him. "You're not gonna get rid of me by trying to scare me off. I've never walked away from a fight —"

"Jane," Dave interrupted, "listen to me for a change. You've gone too far this time. Light will come after you with blood in his eye. If you want to stay alive to collect our bet, you'll leave." He added, "Besides, right now I'm in no shape to keep my end of the bargain . . . if you know what I mean."

Her eyes widened. "You mean those bastards did some kind of permanent damage to you —"

"No, no," Dave said, "I'll be all right. But I need some time. And you need to disappear. When things cool down and I'm feeling better, I'll pay up. You won't be disappointed. I give you my word on that."

Her expression softened. "Oh, Dave . . ."

"Don't start that," he said. "Just promise me you'll leave Creede tonight, right away. Send me a telegram when you get to where you're going. I'll be along."

As though this was too good to be true, she said, "You wouldn't welsh on a bet, would you?"

"On my honor as a gambling man," Dave said, raising his right hand. He might have been taking an oath before witnesses. "I'm serious, Jane. Get out of here tonight. Don't tarry."

"Dave," she whispered, "you care about me, don't you? You really do, deep down in your heart —"

Dave waved her quiet and pointed to the cabin door. "If you care about me, you'll get a move on."

Calamity Jane grinned. Her cheeks grew rosy. "All right, I'm going. I'll ride fast and hard . . . and I'll be a-waitin' for you."

"Just let me know where you end up," Dave said, "and make sure it's a long way from here."

Calamity Jane was too flustered to speak, like a schoolgirl in love. Suddenly conscious of others in the room, she blushed. Turning away, she went to the door in long strides.

Molly met her there. She held out her hand. "Thank you, Jane."

Their eyes met and their hands clasped tightly together. Calamity Jane said, "You know, you're not so bad." Then she opened the door, took a last glance back at Dave, and disappeared into the night.

Molly closed the door and moved across the room to the kitchen table and the two men sitting there.

"I'd like to know more about this bet you made," she said.

Dave shook his head, grimacing as he exhaled. "That's between Jane and me."

The silence that followed was broken by Roger, who looked admiringly at the gambler. "First time I ever saw a man throw a woman out and make her love him for it."

Dave cast a critical look at the young man.

"Dave Hughes," Molly said, "whatever that wager was about, you'd better keep your word with her. I saw you make a solemn promise. You're not off the hook just because you convinced her to leave."

The gambler made no reply. Instead, he looked up at her and said, "You'll have to get out of Creede, too. Light's deputies and Drago's henchmen will be hunting you with orders to shoot on sight."

"I don't leave a job half-finished," Molly

said. "When my investigation is complete, I'll turn in my report. Then I'll leave."

"As far as I'm concerned," Dave said, "your work is completed."

Molly smiled. "I know you're trying to protect me from harm, but —"

"Roger will get you a saddle horse," he interrupted. "You can head for Alamosa tonight and catch the train there tomorrow or the next day."

"Dave," Molly said, "I appreciate what you're trying to do, but I'm not leaving. Not until I've finished my work here."

"And I'm telling you your work is finished," he said. "You're fired."

XXII

Molly saw that he was serious. As far as he was concerned, the discussion had ended. It was beyond arguing.

"I'm the one who put Sharon in danger," Molly said. "I can't leave here with that on my conscience."

"Don't worry," Dave said. "I'll protect her. I'm not going to let Drago lay a hand on her."

"You're injured," Molly said. "How can you protect her now?"

"How can you?" he snapped back at her. "You got yourself locked up in one of Drago's saloons, then you were thrown in jail. Now that you're an escaped prisoner, you'll probably be gunned down next time you walk down Creede Avenue."

"I'll take my chances," Molly said.

"You ran out of chances a long time ago," Dave said. "You can't do any good here. You might as well admit that and get out of this district." He added, "While you're still able."

Molly's face heated. Dave glared at her. This was a stalemate. While Molly had no intention of relenting, she realized she could never win this dispute with a frontal attack. At last she exhaled and said, "All right, Dave. I'll leave."

The gambler's battered and bruised face relaxed. "It's for your own good. If anything happened to you . . ."

All the while Roger had watched in silence. Now he pushed his chair back from the table and stood. "Don't you worry about Sharon," he said. "Between the two of us we'll look out for her."

Molly asked, "You plan to move against Drago?"

"No," Dave said, "we're outnumbered and outgunned."

Roger moved toward the door. "Dave, I'll run up to the livery and get a horse for her."

"Make that a horse and top buggy," he said. To Molly, he added, "You'll have to get through Creede tonight, and on horseback you'll draw attention. Too many people know you by sight, and with the top up on a buggy, you might not be seen."

After Roger was gone, Dave said, "I spoke harshly to you a minute ago. I want to apologize. You've done everything I asked, and more, even risked your life for me. I'm grateful." He held out his hand.

Molly grasped his outstretched hand.

"No hard feelings?" he asked.

"No hard feelings," she replied.

"Good," he said. "When you reach Denver, send a message by wire so we'll know you're all right."

Molly knew Dave was worried about her in exactly the same way she was concerned about Sharon. The same weight of responsibility was on his shoulders. The irony of this situation almost brought a smile to her face. She could not resist agreeing to his request by saying, "Like Calamity Jane, you haven't heard the last of me."

A pained expression came to his face. "You would have to remind me."

Molly gazed at him for a long moment. "I've already said my piece about her, but before I go I'd like to say something else. Call it parting advice."

"I reckon you've earned the right," Dave said. "What is it?"

"You know what they say about a woman scorned," Molly said. "If you think Calamity Jane was enraged that time she came after you with a knife —"

Dave interrupted, "I know what you're going to say. You're going to tell me that I haven't seen anything yet."

"Something like that," Molly said. "That woman's in love with you, and you've sent her some mixed signals."

"You women stick together in matters of the heart, don't you?" he asked.

Molly shrugged. "That's my advice. Take it for what it's worth."

"You're right," Dave said, meeting her gaze. "This time I'll keep my word with her." He paused. "I'm just glad I didn't wager a marriage license."

Molly smiled. "I'd still like to know what it was you did wager."

"I don't want to talk about it," he said.

In ten minutes Molly bid him good-bye when Roger returned with the horse and buggy. She again promised to let them know when she reached Denver.

Lamplight spilled outside when Molly opened the cabin door. She saw the horse out there, a deep-chested gelding, black as the night with three white socks. The animal was harnessed to a high-wheeled buggy with a canvas top.

Roger followed her outside. "Leave the rig at the livery in Wagon Wheel Gap. The livery here in Upper Creede has an exchange agreement with them."

Molly climbed in and sat on the leather-covered seat. She took up the reins. Out of the corner of her eye she saw Dave hobble into the doorway and raise his hand in a parting gesture. Molly smiled at him and waved back.

"Well, so long," Roger said. "I've never met anyone quite like you, Molly. Been a pleasure knowing you."

"Good-bye, Roger," Molly said. She urged the horse away, drove out to the road, and turned toward Creede. She was glad for the darkness. She felt guilty for her deceit. Dave and Roger were thoroughly convinced that she was on her way out of town.

A cold wind swept down the canyon, rustling the canvas top of the buggy. Molly was protected from the wind's chill, and when she sat back in the seat her face was nearly concealed from view.

Ahead she heard the sounds of rowdy nightlife in Creede. A glow of light from lamps and lanterns came into view, then as she rounded a bend at the mouth of the canyon she saw the boxy, false-fronted buildings of Creede.

Molly drove down Creede Avenue amid the few wagons and horsebackers on the street. Boardwalks were jammed, and several times men dashed across the street in front of her. She drove past the Orleans Club and other establishments. No one gave her second notice, and while she reached the Wall Street intersection confident that she had not been seen, she found she was perspiring as though she had just run a gauntlet.

She turned left at the side street and headed for the Fifth Avenue Hotel. The street was dark and empty.

Molly tied the black horse at the rail outside the grand hotel. One of the guards opened the door for her, and she strode across the lobby to the desk and matter-of-factly asked for her room key.

Once the night clerk recognized her, he seemed vastly relieved. Evidently the management had been in a quandary about what to do with her belongings. Surely there had been a terrible mistake in her arrest, and for the time being the lock had been repaired and her clothes and other belongings had been left intact — completely undisturbed, the clerk assured her.

Molly thanked the clerk, took her key, and climbed the stairs to her room. Yes, there had been a terrible mistake, one that she intended to make Marshal John Light remember. But first she would go after Lou Drago.

In her room, Molly undressed and took a sponge bath, trying her best to soap away the jailhouse stench, which seemed to have permeated not only her clothes but her flesh. She scrubbed until her skin was pink.

Molly changed into her divided riding skirt and a dark blouse, the outfit that gave her the most freedom of movement. She checked the loads of her weapons, then strapped the derringer to her right thigh and thrust the Colt Lightning Model .38 revolver into her shoulder holster. Then she put on the light jacket that covered the gun.

A wave of dizziness swept over her and Molly realized she was weak with hunger. She left the room and went downstairs to the hotel dining room. She ordered a steak dinner and wolfed down three pieces of French bread while she waited for the meal.

At this late hour the dining room was quiet. With white tablecloths and folded napkins, china and silver service, and sparkling crystal chandeliers overhead, the room possessed genuine elegance. It was a world apart from the dangers outside.

In these civilized surroundings Molly wondered if she was making a mistake. Perhaps she should return to Denver as soon as possible. It was not too late. She could file her report with U.S. Marshal Saul Philips. Let the law handle this one, and both Drago and Light would be brought to justice.

Maybe, and maybe not. Her testimony alone might not be enough. Drago had been in scrapes with the law before and come through unscathed. In all likelihood he would be able to pull it off again.

Molly ate ravenously, finishing the meal with a piece of apple pie and coffee. When she drank the last of the coffee from the delicate cup of white china, she made her decision. She could not abandon Sharon. And she could not leave a job unfinished.

She left the Fifth Avenue Hotel and drove the buggy back up Creede Avenue. A pair of Light's deputies crossed the street in front of her, but paid no attention to her as she sat back in the shadows of the buggy. She pulled off the street on the far side of the hotel next door to the Orleans Club, a building that stood at the mouth of the canyon.

She sat there a few minutes until she was certain no one was around, then got out. She moved swiftly to the rear of the hotel and followed the alley to the back door of the Orleans Club.

By starlight she saw that the rear entrance to the club was at the top of a short flight of stairs. Molly eased up the steps, pausing when a loose board creaked underfoot. Caution was hardly necessary, though, as noise from Creede Avenue covered the sounds she made.

In the darkness Molly found the door

handle. She was not surprised when she discovered it was locked. Her fingertips went to the keyhole below the handle, then she reached into her handbag and brought out her ring of master skeleton keys. She fumbled with them, trying one after another in the lock, until the right key released the latch.

Returning the keys to her handbag, Molly turned the door handle and slowly opened the door, remembering that this one squealed on its hinges. She had heard it the night she'd followed Sharon to her cabin. But at this time of night the raucous sounds from Creede Avenue again drowned out the noise she made. She slipped into the back hallway of the Orleans Club and closed the door behind her.

She was in a storeroom. Looking around, she saw beer barrels and crates. This storeroom, she realized, ran along one wall of the gambling parlor and directly behind the bar in the saloon. No lamp was lighted in here, but light seeped through cracks in the wall and around a doorframe that opened off the saloon. Molly headed for it.

Sounds of voices from the saloon made a steady hum in this room, but as Molly came close to the door she heard another, bleating sound. She stopped, trying to identify it. Long ago she had heard the sounds of a

242

dying rat caught in a trap, and this strange noise reminded her of it.

On the floor off to her left she saw movement. Startled, she reached for her revolver. But before she drew it, she realized she was seeing someone lying there, bound hand and foot. She rushed toward that helpless figure and knelt down, recognizing Sharon.

XXIII

Molly loosened the thick, mildewed bar towel that gagged Sharon's mouth. When she took it off, Sharon sputtered frantically before she was able to make sense.

"Molly . . . get out . . . he's . . . he's coming back. . . ."

"Shhhh," Molly said, calming her. "I'll take you out of here. Then we'll worry about Drago." She untied the knotted lengths of cord that bound Sharon's wrists and ankles, then helped the young woman stand.

Sharon's feet were numb and she almost fell. Molly grabbed her. But just as she got an arm under her, the door to the saloon opened with a burst of sound and light.

Lou Drago came into the storeroom carrying a glass lamp. Molly saw him first, but could not free her arm from Sharon in time to reach for her revolver. In that fraction of a second Drago saw her. He recovered from his surprise fast enough to shift the lamp to his left hand and draw his gun with his right.

Now he came toward them, his teeth showing through his dark beard in a grin or

244

a snarl. "Well, whatta you know. Now I got me two bitches."

Sharon cursed him. "What're you going to do, beat us up like you beat my father? You stinking coward!"

"Shut up," Drago said mildly. "Your mouth has already gotten you in enough trouble."

Sharon turned to Molly. "When I found out you were in jail, I told him —"

"You threatened me," Drago interrupted with a harsh laugh, "threatened to send me to prison for the rest of my life, didn't you?" He waved the gun at her. "No bitch threatens me, and you two have come to the end of the line."

"If anything happens to either one of us," Molly said, "federal lawmen will come after you."

He smirked at her. "Thanks to your young friend here, I know all about you now. I know why you came here and who you're working for. Lady, you should have left town when I invited you to leave." He grinned again. "Now I'm gonna have my fun with you. Turn around, both of you. Put your hands behind your backs —"

"No!" Sharon yelled, lunging at Drago. Her hands clawed out in front of her.

Drago was too surprised to react immediately, but he got a shot off just as Sharon leaped on him. Driven back, the lamp fell from his hand.

Molly was momentarily paralyzed by surprise at Sharon's suicidal leap straight into the revolver clenched in Drago's hand, and she watched in horror. The gunshot thundered in the storeroom. Molly saw the lamp fall to the floor, where it burst. Shards of glass cascaded out like a shower of diamonds, and tongues of flame licked at the spreading pool of kerosene.

In that instant — one that seemed painfully long but in fact lasted only a second or two — Molly regained her senses and rushed at Drago. He was struggling to keep his balance against the momentum of Sharon's lunge. Molly grabbed his gun hand. She tried to pull him away from Sharon, twisting his wrist around at the same time, when a gust of heat swept up her thighs. She realized her skirt was on fire.

Suddenly bright flames danced all around. Her legs were burning. She let go of Drago and instinctively dropped to the floor. Rolling, she beat her hands against the fabric of her riding skirt. Her nostrils and mouth filled with smoke. She choked.

Molly knew with sudden, terrifying clarity that the billowing smoke would kill her more quickly than fire. Blindly dragging herself, she half-crawled across the floor. Tears washed down her face. She could see nothing but the dim light of flames some-where behind her. She felt for the back door, crying and choking as she moved with nightmarish slowness.

At last she came up against a vertical sur-face. Coughing, she reached for the door handle. Hand frantically searching, she touched hot metal . . . grasped the door handle . . . hand burning. . . .

Consciousness slipped away. She sank against the door, unable to breathe. In the distance she heard a scream . . . panicked shouts . . . .

"Fire! Fire!"

"My God! The town's on fire!"

Only later would Molly realize that she had turned that door handle, searing her hand. Her weight had pushed the door open. Partially revived by the cool night air, she dragged herself outside and rolled down the back steps of the Orleans Club.

The gust of fresh air from the open door fueled the smoldering storeroom fire into a furnace of raging flames. To escape, Molly dragged herself across the alley into the high weeds growing up the bank of Willow Creek. She collapsed.

Sounds of gurgling water came into her ears like soothing music from afar. She opened her eyes to a pale sky overhead, slowly realizing that day had dawned, slowly realizing she was alive. Sitting up, Molly blinked as she looked around. She awoke to a charred world. The first light of day was hazy with the smoldering ruins of Creede's business district.

Molly rose up to her knees. She stared in disbelief at the sight before her. The heart of the mining camp was gone. All the saloons and gambling parlors, all the hotels and banks and other businesses jammed side by side in those false-fronted frame buildings on Creede Avenue, were reduced to tangled heaps of burned timbers and blackened stone foundations. Amid the wisps of smoke rising from those charred remains Molly saw businessmen poking through the ruins for anything that had not been consumed. Huddled on Creede Avenue were many groups of men, homeless and strangely quiet.

"Hey, lady, you all right?"

Molly turned and saw a man coming down the alley. His face and hands were black with ashes. He was hatless and his hair was tangled. Molly struggled to her feet, and coughed as she tried to reply.

"You been out here all night?" he asked.

248

Molly nodded as he came to her. Her gaze went to the burned-out Orleans Club. "I think . . . someone may have died. . . ."

"No, lady, everybody got out of the Orleans Club alive," he said. "Funny thing is, no bodies have been found a'tall. That fire went fast. Wind caught it, you know. We've been hunting all night, and looks like nobody got killed. Guess we missed you in the dark."

"Drago was in there," Molly said.

"Yes, ma'am, but he got out," the man said. "Saw him myself. He was helping a young lady out of there, last I saw." He paused. "Fought that damned fire all night. Just went too fast, that's all. Too damned fast."

He looked at her again. "Lady, you all right?"

Molly nodded. She was at once relieved and apprehensive about what he had said about Lou Drago. What did that mean? He had helped Sharon out of the burning building? Or was she injured — shot — and he was only making his escape in the confusion of the raging fire?

When the man was gone, Molly turned around and looked down the length of the alley. The Fifth Avenue Hotel, that grand brick edifice, now stood alone on Wall

Street. The other buildings, including Dr. Simms's office, were gone. So was the ornate San Juan Building. Now from this back alley Molly could see all the way across town to the train depot, her view unobstructed. The depot was a steep-roofed building constructed of stone blocks.

Remembering the buggy, Molly quickly turned around. It was gone. Either the horse had run off or the vehicle had been stolen. That thought stuck in her mind. She tried to visualize what might have happened last night. If Drago had gone that way, away from the fire and away from the center of the mining camp, he would have taken Sharon straight toward the place where she had left the top buggy.

Taking a deep breath to clear both her head and her lungs, Molly walked up the alley, rounding the corner at the charred remains of the hotel that had stood next to the Orleans Club. Even though this two-story structure was upwind from the fire's point of origin, it had evidently been close enough to ignite. The second floor had caved in, and now smoke rose from burned spring mattresses and heaps of blankets and pillows.

From there Molly walked out to the street. She looked down the length of Creede Avenue, unable to take her eyes from the scene of destruction. The devastation was utterly complete and it shocked her senses, made her feel aimless, without purpose.

Everyone else must have felt the same way. She saw people wandering in the street as though dazed. Men stood in small groups, looking around dumbly. A group of children leaned over the edge of a blackened foundation, peering down into a basement that was filled with charred remains.

Just as Molly's gaze went to those children, a voice boomed out of the basement. The children turned and ran, sprinting down Creede Avenue toward a block of residences that had escaped the flames. Molly immediately recognized the crazed voice, and then she saw a lean, top-hatted figure emerge from the depths of the basement.

"This camp called Creede has been destroyed by the sword of the Almighty!" Preacher Ed called out. "The flaming sword of the Almighty has swept away the squalid dens of sinners. Look around you, infidels. See the power of the Almighty. See the power! Read Genesis, chapter nineteen! Read of Sodom! Read of Gomorrah! All you sinners will know the fires of hell for all eternity! Repent! Repent, you sinners! You! Yes, you! And you! And you!" With this last shout he pointed a knobby finger straight at Molly.

One of the sinners called out, "Find any money down there, preacher?"

The question brought ridiculing laughter. Another man called out, "All the money in that safe down there was burned to ashes. Talk about a hot fire from hell!"

Molly realized then that the Merchants & Miners Bank had stood there. And the sight of Preacher Ed stepping out onto the street made her think of the jail. The county courthouse across the street and down half a block still stood. Other buildings over there had also escaped the flames. Now Molly wondered why she had not seen Marshal John Light.

She looked around for the lanky lawman while an argument raged between Preacher Ed and several of his detractors. Strange, she thought, that he was not here, aiding the townspeople. Her thoughts were interrupted by shrill blasts of a steam engine. The people on Creede Avenue turned toward that sound, then moved as one to the depot. Molly guessed that a relief train was coming, bringing medical supplies, food, and water from Alamosa.

A renewed sense of urgency surged through her. She turned her back on the burned-out camp and hurried to the spot beside the hotel where she had left the top buggy last night.

The ground was covered with black soot and a dusting of white ashes that had been blown into small heaps and eddies by the night wind. She searched the ground for tracks. In the ashes she saw a profusion of bootprints obviously made by men who had fought the fire. The ashes would have covered any tracks left by the buggy.

She moved out beyond the fringe of ashes. In the dirt she saw horse tracks and a set of thin lines. Those lines imprinted in the soil had been left by a high-wheeled buggy. Her theory that Drago might have come this way when he escaped the burning Orleans Club took on more promise when she trailed the wheel marks out to the freight road that led into Willow Creek Canyon.

Molly walked rapidly, half-running, up the canyon road. The trail of the iron-tired wheels, while intermittent, was not difficult to follow. Overhead, the band of sky between the canyon walls was brightening with the first rays of the morning sun.

The promise of a bright, cheery day was false. Molly knew that when she reached Upper Creede and rounded the corner of the long boardinghouse. She saw the cabin. The door stood open. Inside, she saw an overturned chair.

The chair lay on its back in an elongated rectangle of morning light that streamed in through the open door. Molly burst in, gun drawn, dreading what she might find.

She saw immediately that a mighty struggle had taken place in the small room. The pine table was askew, dishes were scattered about, and across the room the mattress was half off the bed. A pair of bare feet stuck out from under it.

Molly rushed over and pulled the mattress away from the still figure. It was Roger. She saw a swollen welt on the side of his head as she bent over him.

"Roger," she whispered, not knowing if he was alive, "can you hear me?"

"Well, look who showed up."

Molly whirled around, at once recognizing the voice of the man who had eased into the doorway behind her. Sammy's long shadow stretched across the floor in front of him. The small man wore a three-piece suit and a black bowler. In his little hand the revolver he held looked enormous. He waved it at Molly.

"Lou told me I just might catch you here if I waited around," Sammy said. "He was right, wasn't he?"

"Where did he take Sharon?" Molly asked. "Where's Dave?"

Sammy snorted. "You ask more damned questions." He stepped into the cabin, aiming his gun point-blank at her. "Asking questions right up to the last. It's all over for you. Here's what you get for whipping me —"

Molly saw his expression tighten. She dropped a shoulder and rolled just as he pulled the trigger. The blast of the revolver filled the room with sound that reverberated in Molly's ears and acrid powder smoke that stung her nostrils.

She made a complete roll and came up with her .38 in front of her. In that fraction of a second she saw Sammy frantically take aim at the moving target she presented. She fired just as he got off a second shot.

Her bullet caught Sammy at the base of the neck and sent him stumbling backward. He coughed wetly, and the wound at his throat blossomed bright red. He fell out through the doorway, his dark beady eyes stretched open in disbelief.

Molly stood up. Only then was she certain that his bullet had missed. She saw a plowed groove in the plank floor inches away from where she had lain.

Roger was unconscious. Molly discovered that when she saw his chest heaving slightly. She pulled and lifted him onto the mattress on the floor. After examining his head wound again, she agonized over her next decision. Roger needed treatment by a doctor, but she couldn't spare the time to go after Simms. She had to leave — now.

She left the cabin, stepping over the body of Sammy. Eyes still open, the corpse stared straight up at the bright blue sky of morning.

Molly found Sammy's horse tied beside the cabin. She took the reins and swung up, noting that the stirrups were just about the right length for her. Urging the horse out to the road, she turned and rode through Upper Creede at a high lope. Now she didn't bother to look for the wheel tracks left by the top buggy. She knew where Drago had gone.

Molly rode past the buildings of the ore-reduction mill above Upper Creede. Her theory about Drago was confirmed when she saw thin ruts angling off the freight road to join the old mining road that switchbacked up the mountainside. Carrying three passengers, the buggy left a distinct trail.

Molly fought her instinct to dig her heels into the horse and run him as hard and fast as he would go up the steep-sided mountain.

She knew she must save the animal's strength for the long climb ahead. Nothing would be gained by running the horse into the ground.

Still, her sense of urgency was almost overwhelming. In a deliberate pace the horse made his way up the switchback road, saddle leather creaking, bridle chain clinking. The slow progress gave ample time for Molly's mind to fill with dark thoughts. She could not shake the fear that she was too late.

At the top of the mountain Molly reined the horse to a halt. The animal's breathing was labored. She let him blow. Ahead she saw wheel tracks on the road that led into the pine trees.

If this climb was slow for her on horseback, she thought, it had been even slower for three people in a one-horse buggy. Molly wondered how many hours Drago was ahead of her. *No way of knowing* was the only answer that came to her, and then she rode on, entering the forest.

When she reached the edge of the trees at the clearing, she abruptly drew rein. Across the grassy clearing, the gate that had blocked the road now stood open. Her eyes scanned the treeline over there, alert for movement, a patch of color, anything out of place that would give warning of an ambush.

After a full three minutes of watching, she saw nothing. Birds lazily flew in and out of treetops, and she took that as a sign that no one was over there to frighten them.

Molly touched her heels to the horse. She rode out of the trees and crossed the clearing, aware that the terrain was perfect for an ambush. The sight of slender wheel ruts in the little-used road sent a shiver up her spine. Drago had been here. And he was ahead, somewhere.

But he was not lying in wait in that dense stand of lodgepole pines. No gunshots exploded out of the trees, and Molly reached the open gate safely. She rode through it and followed the road toward the abandoned mine.

When those weathered buildings came into view, she again drew rein. She watched and listened for signs of danger. Then she rode on a short distance, dismounting at the spot where she could leave the weed-grown road and take the shortcut through the forest to the mine shack.

Molly had led the saddle horse only a few yards when she heard another horse whicker. Hers answered with a toss of his head.

She immediately regretted bringing the horse this far. She quickly tied the reins to the nearest tree branch, drew her revolver, and bent low as she ran, moving to her right toward a thicket. Drago might not have heard her horse, but she could hardly afford to wait and find out. With this man she did not expect a second chance. One mistake on her part was all he needed to gain the edge.

Molly ran hard, skidding to her knees behind the thicket, pine cones spraying out in front of her. The leafy branches of the thicket gave her cover. After she caught her breath, she peered around it. The shack was not in sight from here.

Several minutes passed while she watched for movement. The horse stood still where she had left him. No birds sang in the sunny treetops or flitted from bough to bough.

Molly got to her feet and eased out from behind the thicket. She made her way downslope, walking in a direction that would bring her to the shack. A few yards farther, and the back corner of the shack came into sight. Molly stopped again, gun in hand, listening. Then she moved on, one cautious step at a time, pine needles crunching softly under her boots.

She saw the hay manger and pile of stove ashes at the rear of the shack, and as she moved closer, angling to her left, the horse and top buggy came into view. Still in harness, the horse stood with his head drooping, his brown coat caked with dried sweat. A saddle horse was there too.

Molly paused, then left the trees. She approached the shack from its blind side. The horses raised their heads at her approach, but made no sound. She reached the shack and edged around the windowless wall to the front. There, a few feet in front of the door, two figures were on the ground, seated back to back, bound and gagged. They were father and daughter, Dave and Sharon.

With his head bowed, Dave appeared to be unconscious. But Sharon was alert, looking around. When she saw Molly at the side of the shack, her eyes widened. She vigorously shook her head.

"Might as well join the party, detective lady."

Molly was startled by the sound of Lou Drago's voice close behind her. She spun around. Drago leaned against the rear corner of the shack, arms folded casually across his chest. A revolver was thrust through his waistband.

Molly raised her gun, leveling it at him.

"Shoot me," Drago said, "and your friends die." He jerked his head toward a stack of mine timbers thirty yards from the shack.

Molly did not have to look over there to know that she had been drawn into a trap.

Drago was too confident. Now he smirked at her.

Still aiming the .38 at him, she shifted her gaze to the stack of squared timbers. At a signal from Drago, a rifleman stood up behind it. He was John Light. Raising the rifle to his shoulder, he drew a bead on Dave and Sharon.

"Punched a pine knot out of the back wall of this shack," Drago said, "and I watched you come out of the trees. Took your time, didn't you? I could've gunned you down."

"Why didn't you?" Molly asked.

"You're gonna find out," he said, straightening up. "Now hand over your gun." He stepped toward her, hand outstretched.

Molly thumbed back the hammer. "When the shooting starts, you'll go first."

"I ain't gonna buy into that bluff," Drago said. "You ain't the type to shoot a man down." He moved ahead another step.

"This is self-defense," Molly said. "I am the type to protect myself."

Drago halted. "You don't get the picture, do you? Shoot me, and Light's gonna put a bullet in your gambler friend and Sharon. She goes first. Then John'll shoot that tinhorn gambler, and with any luck he'll get you, too. You willing to play this out just for the pleasure of shooting me in cold blood?"

"You're a madman," Molly said.

He snorted. "This is a high-stakes game, lady, the highest. I'm playing for keeps."

"Why?" Molly asked. "Why are you doing this?"

The question angered him. "For a smart lady, you can be as dumb as a post. I set this whole thing up to get you. I figured if you got past Sammy, you'd hightail it up here."

"But why?" Molly asked.

"Dammit!" Drago exclaimed. "It's because of you I got burned out. You wanted to bring me down, and you figured to use Sharon against me. That gambler couldn't get the job done. I showed him. But not you. You kept hounding me, wouldn't quit. Even got some federal lawman after me, didn't you?"

Drago sucked in a deep breath, his eyes flashing with anger. "My fight's with you, detective lady. When I'm through with you, I'm riding outta here. You burned me out, but I'm here to tell you the victory won't be a sweet one." He advanced another step. "The gun, hand it over."

Molly did not lower it. "If I give you my gun, Dave and Sharon go free?"

"That's the deal," he replied.

"How do I know you'll keep your end of it?" Molly asked. "Turn them loose now, and send Light on his way —"

Drago's face reddened with anger. "Gimme that gun."

"I think you're afraid," Molly said, "afraid of a fair fight between the two of us."

"You stinking bitch," he said. "I'll teach you. . . ."

"Like you taught that woman in Denver?" Molly asked.

"She died a slow death," Drago said. "She screamed for death, and I made her suffer for what she done to me."

Molly stared into his eyes, unblinking. She tried to judge if she could shoot him and get a shot off at Light in time to prevent him —

It was too late. Drago turned and raised his hand, giving John Light the signal to shoot.

"Stop," Molly whispered. She lowered her gun.

Drago's mood abruptly changed from anger to delight. He grinned in triumph as he closed the distance between them and snatched the .38 from her hand.

"All right, John," he called out, stepping away from Molly, "shoot them."

Molly had never experienced such rage. Like a volcano, her emotions exploded, blinding her reason. She lunged after Lou Drago with a great leap through the air. He didn't see her coming until the moment before she hit him.

Her momentum knocked the man off his feet. They went down together. As they hit the ground, Molly heard gunshots and recognized the deep booming of a rifle.

Tears streaked down her face while she wrestled with Drago. On top of the flailing man, she had the advantage, and she plowed a knee into his kidney. He gasped, arching his back against the pain, his eyes clenched shut.

Molly raised up. With a powerful chopping blow, she hammered the back of his neck with the side of her hand. Drago fell limp. He lay still. Murderous rage still burning hotly within her, Molly hoped at that moment she had broken his neck.

Through her tears, she glimpsed her .38 on the ground where it had fallen from Drago's hand. The weapon's nickle-plated finish reflected sunlight where it lay gleaming in the dirt like a silvery treasure. Molly lunged for it, expecting at any moment to hear that rifle *boom* again, expecting to feel the slam of a high-powered bullet.

The *boom* did not come, and Molly grabbed up her revolver from the dirt, raising the barrel to take quick aim at the man beside the stack of mine timbers. But John Light was not standing there. He lay sprawled on the ground, hatless now, unmoving.

Molly was amazed. She stared for a long moment, then looked to her right. She expected to see the slumped bodies of Dave and Sharon. Instead she saw them in exactly the same position as before, seated back to back, with Sharon looking at her in alarm.

Molly wondered if she was hallucinating, seeing an imaginary sight that her mind willed her to see. But in the next moment she knew this was real, as the silence was broken by the sound of pine needles crunching under heavy footfalls.

Molly quickly turned and looked into the trees. She saw movement there, an indistinct shape coming toward the treeline. Out of the pine forest waddled a pear-shaped man, Winchester rifle cradled in the crook of one arm. When he emerged from the shadows of the trees, Molly saw that he wore a gray suit and narrow-brimmed hat — city clothes.

When he tipped his head up, Molly recognized him. He was U.S. Marshal Saul Philips.

"You led me on quite a chase this morning, Miss Owens," he said, "and you left a trail of mayhem behind you — a burned-out mining camp and a corpse."

Molly stared at him as he waddled toward her, talking all the way.

"I left Denver as soon as I could after receiving your wire," he said, "and I was able to hitch a ride on that special train bringing relief supplies to Creede. Evidently I got to town just about the time you departed for Upper Creede. Some street-corner preacher remembered seeing you head up the canyon, so I got a horse and rode out."

Philips stopped when he reached her. "At that little cabin I found the remains of Drago's associate, Sammy Jenks, and a miner who was dazed from a knock on the head."

"He's all right?" Molly asked.

Philips nodded. "From talking to him and following horse and buggy tracks, I found my way up here. Looks like I got here in time to lend a hand."

"You did, marshal," Molly said, getting to

266

her feet, "you certainly did. I'll be ever grateful."

Philips replied with a nod of his head, then knelt beside Drago.

Molly turned and rushed to Dave and Sharon. She pulled the handkerchief away from Sharon's mouth.

"Oh, Molly . . . Molly . . ." the young woman said, crying tears of relief and joy.

Molly loosened the twisted wire from Sharon's wrists and ankles, then freed Dave. The gambler was groggy but not unconscious. Molly helped Sharon stretch him out on the ground. She took off her light jacket, folded it, and put it under his head while Sharon shaded his battered face from the sun.

"They beat him, Molly," Sharon said, choking back tears. "Lou beat him, and he said awful things to me. He said he would do things to you and me, and then we'd both die with as much pain as he could give us. Oh, Molly . . ."

"Drago won't hurt anyone," Molly said, looking over her shoulder. Lou Drago was standing now, handcuffed by Marshal Saul Philips. She felt relief, glad that she had not killed him after all. Drago would stand trial, and this time he would not escape justice.

Molly saw Sharon looking down at her father. The young woman lifted her gaze and looked imploringly at Molly. "When I heard you were in jail, I . . . I guess I lost my head. Everything seemed finished. I knew I'd never get my money back . . . Lou could order my father beaten and go free . . . so I went after him, accusing him of everything I could think of." Tears washed down her cheeks.

Molly reached out and stroked her hair, reassuring her that the terror had ended.

"I'm so grateful to you, Molly," Sharon said. "I'll never be able to repay you . . . never."

Molly smiled as she looked at Sharon comforting her father. In the trees behind her she heard a bird singing. Others joined in, greeting the morning sun as it climbed high in a blue sky.

"You already have," Molly said to her.

We hope you have enjoyed this Large Print book. Other Thorndike Press or Chivers Press Large Print books are available at your library or directly from the publishers.

For more information about current and upcoming titles, please call or write, without obligation, to:

Thorndike Press
295 Kennedy Memorial
Waterville, Maine 04901 USA
Tel. (800) 223-1244
Tel. (800) 223-6121

OR

Chivers Press Limited
Windsor Bridge Road
Bath BA2 3AX
England
Tel. (0225) 335336

All our Large Print titles are designed for easy reading, and all our books are made to last.